STOP 2

A Novel

Billie Dureyea Shell

STOP 2

Copyright © 2022

All rights reserved to Billie Dureyea Shell.

No part of this publication may be reproduced, distributed or transmitted in any form or by any means, including photocopying, or other electronic or mechanical methods, without the prior written permission of the publisher, except in the case of brief quotations embodied in critical reviews and certain noncommercial uses permitted by copyright law. Any references to historical events, real people or real places are used factiously. Names, characters, and places are products of the authors imagination.

Front Cover Image By graphic designer
Billie Dureyea Shell & Kenny Writes

First Printing Edition 2022

ISBN 979-8-9866240-1-3

This book is dedicated to:

This Book is dedicated to my nigga SHAWN FARM nigga I told the next one would be 2you keep ur head up nigga we going to get you home........ Just make sure you stop stealing them car antennas cuz them fingers was looks bad LMAO Get at me My Guy..............

Author
Billie Dureyea Shell

Team Shell

ACKNOWLEDGEMENT

This year has really a Mutual Fuckka Co-Vid ain't going nowhere.... But Fucc Co-Vid 19 we ain't going to let it stop NOTHING. So with that let me first and formost give thanks to my heavenly father for making it possible for my family to be okay during this pandemic and for all of us still being here healthy, Lord without you none of this would be possible to my mom I love you with all my heart it's because of you that I'm here and it's because of you that I'll always give 100% , keep my head up and know that I'm the head and not the tail, I love you Momma to my little sister Glenda what's up Blackie I miss you and I love you. To my wife Shatoya thank you for loving me and teaching me how to be more patient I love you with all my heart we got 10 kids you crazy if you think we having another one lol I'm good I got a hold on to the little bit of

Sanity I have left smile plus you drive me crazy enough... To All My Children I love you all and know that y'all the reason that I smile to my uncle Woody I miss you and I love you so much thank you for teaching me how to be a man to my brother Lawrence Mc Cloud I love you thanks always having my back to my brother Fred, I told you I was going to do it, to my sister Needra I miss u and love u little sister Bre I always got u...... to my brother and cousin Zane your missed every hour of every second of every day rest in peace we'll be together soon my nigga I got a few more things I got to do down here. To all my readers in the fans I love you all if it wasn't for y'all my dream couldn't have came true thank you for buying my books and reading them thank you all for letting me know how much y'all appreciate my writing skills and what I do its because of y'all that these books can't stay in stores and I'm going to keep on doing this writing shit as long as y'all wanna read it. With that much I'll let u get to this book I hope you all enjoy it let me know what you think I love all y'all

Author

Billie Dureyea Shell

Chapter 1

SHANICE

"**B**ut I guess forever, doesn't last too long forever Doesn't last too long forever Doesn't last too long these days, hey And I tried to believe that we could make it But trying don't work, so I just have to face that forever Doesn't last too long these days, hey" I listened to Jazmine Sullivan's "Forever Don't Last" as I sat in the parking lot of my building bawling my eyes out. The more I prayed for things to get better in my life the worse things seemed to get. Sharon, my sister? I knew she looked exactly like Tameka, but damn, how could this even be possible? I grabbed my cell phone to call my grandmother. I trusted her and knew she wouldn't lie to me, but as I stared down at the number, I knew this could possibly bring news I didn't want to hear, as well as show me that even the people who've loved you since birth will lie to you. "Hello." I heard my grandmother's voice and I knew I had to respond immediately, otherwise she'd hang up. "Grandma, it's Shannie," I said through my tears. "Do you know what time it is?" I looked at the clock on my dash and it was only 7:30. "It's not that late, Grandma." I was already irritated and I hadn't even begun asking questions yet. "Well, I'm in the bed, what you need child?" I rolled my eyes. My grandmother could be the sweetest old lady you ever did come across, but sometimes she was a pain. I hadn't talked to her in a few weeks so you'd think she'd be happy to hear from me, but I knew how she was and I knew this conversation would have to wait until I could go over to her house because she really wasn't trying to be on the phone right now. "I just wanted to tell you I love you, and I'll be by there tomorrow," I lied. "Okay, baby, I love you, too. Goodnight." She hung up before I could say goodnight. I turned the song back up and listened to it on repeat about a dozen times. Maxwell was the only man I wanted, but how could I be with him now, knowing he was having a child with my sister – a sister I borderline hated? "Oh my God!" I put my hand over my chest as my heart began to beat faster than its normal pace. I was startled out of my sleep by Max knocking on my window. I looked at the clock and it was now 11:45, I couldn't believe I'd fallen asleep in the car listening to "Forever Don't Last" on replay. I rolled down the window and looked at him. I could see the sadness in his eyes that had been there ever since we'd broken up. "What do you want, Max?" I gave him my coldest stare. "I've been sitting in front of your front door all night waiting on you to get out of the damn car and you want to have an attitude? I don't know why I try! I don't know why anybody tries, one nigga screws you over and you act like we're all bad!" He went off like I'd called his mama out of her name or something. "I didn't ask you to follow me home or sit outside my door." I rolled my eyes. "You're right, you didn't. But I came to make sure you were, okay considering all that happened tonight, but since you're trying to act like you have it all together, I'm going to leave you to your little feelings. I don't know why I keep coming back for the bullshit." He walked away shaking his head and didn't even look back. I knew I was hurting him, but I was in no position to allow him or anyone else to be there for me. I just needed answers. I sent Dan a quick text to call me, since I knew a lot of this was because of his mother. I felt maybe he'd be able to tell me why she was doing this to me. I'd let Dan go, so why was Miss Harris still trying to ruin my life?

Chapter 2

DANDRIDGE

I changed into some dry clothes, and looked at the shiner Maxwell had given me. I couldn't believe everything that had just taken place at my mother's dinner party! Me and my best friend were done because of a girl, the one thing we'd said would never come between us. Bros before hoes was always the motto! But the thing was, Shanice definitely wasn't a hoe and I couldn't believe Maxwell would do this to me. He was such a standup guy; I knew I'd have to pull out all the stops for Shanice to ultimately pick me. I also couldn't believe Shanice and Sharon were sisters! Leave it to my mother to figure some shit like that out! I walked downstairs where my mother was telling everyone goodbye and giving a bogus apology about how things turned out. She'd set this whole thing up and had unknowingly set me up in her efforts to make Shanice miserable. I watched her hug Maxwell's mother, smiling in her face like she wasn't doing foul shit to that woman's son and Lord knows I prayed Maxwell never got his mother involved because I didn't believe my mom could beat her if it came down to it and that lady did not play about Max. The things that could come between best friends, I shook my head at the thought. "What are you doing, Ma?" I asked once the house was clear. "I have no idea what you're talking about," she said in a patronizing tone. "Please don't play with me, Ma. Where you'd get the sperm?" I asked a question I already knew the answer to. "Sperm? Boy, what are you talking about? Don't beat around the bush!" I hated how my mother always had to make people spell things out for her. She always had to know you knew something for a fact before she'd ever confess to it. "Sharon told me she used artificial insemination to get pregnant and it was guaranteed that the sperm belonged to Maxwell. I know you have some friends in very high places, how'd you get it?" I gave her a look I'd only given to Shanice and Cecelia when I was beyond angry with them, and she knew that even though she was the parent, I still meant business.

"I did my research, went on a couple of dates with Dillon Granger the owner of the sperm clinic Maxwell's sperm was held at and, well, let's just say I owe Dillon a favor." She sounded like Cruella as she spoke. "It wasn't Maxwell's sperm." I shook my head because ever since my conversation with Sharon, I really wanted to break down and cry. I didn't donate sperm to ever know the names of the women who used it or know the children who came from it. "Excuse me?" My mother lifted a brow to indicate her interest in what I was saying. "You heard me! It wasn't his! Now you've screwed me over and I have two kids on the way! What am I going to do with two more kids, when I didn't want any at all?" I yelled at her, and felt tears roll down my cheeks. I hadn't even realized I'd gotten that emotional. "Now I have to tell Shanice this shit and I'll never get her back! What am I divorcing Cecelia for, if not to be with Shanice?" My mother looked at me as if I weren't even talking. She didn't step toward me to console me, she just looked at me. "You don't care who you ruin, all because you want to hurt Shanice so damn bad." "Humph." She smirked. "You will not say a word," she said, again sounding like Cruella. "I will not keep your secrets! I've lied enough." I stuck out my chest as if to let her know she was talking to a grown ass man. "You will keep this secret. You will not tell Shanice or anybody else what you just told me. I don't know how you and Max did it and I don't care to know any of the details. All I do know is that you will not open your mouth, is that understood?" Her voice was ice cold, she almost sounded psychotic. "And if I tell them?" "You will regret it." She walked away and I knew she meant exactly what she said. My phone started to vibrate and Shanice's named popped up on the screen. I need to talk to you, call me, was all the text said and I knew my mother had just put me in a position to lie to her all over again.

Chapter 3

LA'DRAYSHA

43 Years ago

"No, please don't make me go!" I begged Miss Betty Mae with tears streaming down my cheeks. She was the only foster parent I'd had that actually cared about me and I didn't want to go to another home, I wanted to stay with her. "You have to go, baby, your time here with me is up." She tried to pull my hands from her shirt as I held on for dear life. I loved her and her daughter Melissa. They were both so loving and nice to me. I was twelve-years-old. Melissa was only two years older than I was, and she was definitely the big sister I'd always wanted but never got. Miss Betty Mae lived in a small house in what most considered the projects, but not much happened on the side she lived on. Everyone loved and respected her because she was a good Christian lady and her daughter Melissa was very respectful. She had three foster kids, including me, and she loved us all like we were her own, but I felt like she loved me more. She spent so much one on one time with me, but now she was willing to just let me go. I'd been in foster care since I was five years old, separated from my older brothers who were twelve and sixteen at the time. Our mother was murdered by our father's wife after she'd shown up at their doorstep demanding he leave her and come home to us. His wife had no idea he'd been having a sixteen-year affair with my mother, so that very night after all hell had broken loose at their house, she decided to show up at our house and as soon as my mother opened the door, she shot her and walked away calmly like she hadn't done a thing. I was standing right behind her. I saw my mother's body drop to the floor like a ragdoll as blood spilled from her head onto the hardwood floor she'd just cleaned earlier that day. I couldn't move as I looked down at her motionless body, her eyes still opened as if she were just staring up at the ceiling. I was in complete shock as my brothers both ran past me, almost knocking me down to get to her, their cries loud as they called her name, wishing, praying that she'd answer, she didn't. Seeing it made me numb; not only was I glued to the spot I stood in, but I couldn't cry or react, I was a statue. One of our neighbors, Miss Suzanne, heard the gunshot and called the police. She came over and took me and brothers to her house so we wouldn't have to be in the house with our mother's body on floor at the front door. A few days later we were told by the social worker our father didn't want us, and because they couldn't locate any living relatives for us, he'd signed us over to the state. I never saw my brothers again, but I promised myself I'd find them one day if they didn't find me first. "You said you loved me!" I cried. "I do love you, La'Draysha." She bent down to speak to me. "You knew this would be temporary, I can't adopt any of you as much as I would love to, but I hear you're going to a nice permanent home." A tear fell from her eye, but I didn't believe she cared. "If you make me leave, I'll always remember this and never forgive you." I threatened her with the hope she'd change her mind, but she only nodded to the social workers, giving them the okay to take me away. I kicked and screamed as a lady picked me up and put me into the backseat of an old grey sedan. I looked out of the window and Melissa was waving goodbye, but she didn't look sad at all. Miss Betty Mae tapped her on the shoulder and they walked back into the house, not even looking at me. "They'll pay for this," I whispered under my breath as the view of the house disappeared behind me. **(Present Day)** I walked back downstairs to apologize to Dan for my attitude. I couldn't believe what he'd just told me. I had plans for Shanice and her family, and Dan continued to get in my way because of his little feelings for that goody-two-shoes. I didn't raise my son to be so caught up in his feelings, and I knew he didn't get it from his father. I approached the end of the staircase and heard Dan's voice just loud enough that I didn't have to take another step. "There are so many things I want to tell you, but I can't," I heard him say. "Just know that I love you so much and I'm sorry for everything I've put you through. I know, I know. I understand, but I really need a chance to show you that I'm for real. I won't hurt you again, just let me be there for you!" I'd heard enough. "Hang up the damn phone." I approached him with even more attitude than I had before. He glared, but didn't dare test me. "I'll you call you back," he told Shanice. "Leave that girl alone, Dandridge! Go home, apologize to your wife, and make things right with her. Do not let Cecelia get back on a plane to Spain with my grandbaby. You fix your marriage!" His nose flared up and jaw clinched tight like he had something he wanted to say to me. "Is there something on your mind, son?" I tested him. "No, there's nothing on my mind." He cut his eyes at me and, if looks could kill, I'd be as dead as my mother. "Bye," he said as he grabbed his hoodie off the chair. "I love you," I told him in a sweeter tone. "Humph. Yeah okay," he responded and walked out of the door. Dan had no idea who Shanice was and the plans I had in store. When I made promises to myself, I always kept them, and when I said Betty Mae and Melissa would pay, I meant it. I just hated that my son had gotten caught in the crossfire.

Chapter 4
MAXWELL

The ride back home seemed to take so long. I hated Dan and his mother for making things so difficult for not only Shanice, but for me as well. I wanted to give that girl everything Dan refused to give her, and more, but she was too blinded by all the drama to see it. I never much agreed with Dan's ways, but he was still my boy, like my brother, and I'd officially given that up tonight. I gave up my good title as a loyal friend trying to be with the woman that I felt was the love of my life, and she kept toying with me as if her feelings were the only ones which mattered. "How selfish," I thought. "What could Miss Harris even have on Shanice that's so bad she wants to ruin this girl and everybody she comes in contact with?" It was time I did some digging. If finding out Miss Harris's motives was the thing that would bring me and Shanice together, it was exactly what I'd do. "So what the hell do you want... uh baby What the hell do you want... from me What the hell do you want... I need to know What the hell do you want... baby What the hell do you want from me" I heard 112 singing their song "What the hell do you want", which was the ringtone I had set for Sharon, and I rolled my eyes. I was so tired of her. I didn't know how many different ways you could tell someone to go away. I pressed the ignore button because I was never in the mood to deal with her and I definitely didn't know why she was calling me at almost one in the morning. I heard the ringer again and decided to put my phone on "do not disturb", and threw it over in the passenger seat. I just hoped nothing happened at work in the middle of the night where I'd be needed because, with the Army, you never really know when you're going to get a call. I walked into my house and looked around. It was so empty, when it was once filled with love. I know I'd only experienced that love for a little over a month, but it felt like Shanice and I had spent years in the house together. I shook my head, trying to get rid of the thoughts, but I knew I wouldn't stop thinking about her. This was one time I wished I could be cradled by my mother and assured everything would be alright. But instead I just began to pray. God brought Shanice to me one time, I was sure he could do it again.

Chapter 5

DANDRIDGE

I closed my front door behind me and leaned against it for a moment. I sighed hard because I knew I had to deal with Cecelia and try my best to do what my mother asked of me. I was tired of letting her control my life, but when my mom set her mind to making someone regret a decision, she literally had no bounds or limits and I just realized that it went for anyone. I didn't know how one person could be so evil. "I'll be gone tomorrow," Cecelia said when she looked up at me standing in the doorway. She was packing her things and I could tell she'd been crying. I closed my eyes for a second and exhaled as I silently gave myself a motivational speech on how I could talk her into staying. I walked over to her and grabbed her hand off of a stack of clothes. "Don't go. I've been a jerk, and I'm sorry." "Where is this coming from, Dan? Your mother?" She looked at me in disbelief. "No it's not coming from my mother. It's coming from me. I'm sorry. I didn't bring you all the way to the States just to leave you or send you back home." I hated lying to her, but it seemed that lying was all I was capable of nowadays and, no matter how much I wanted to get it right, I couldn't. "So why all of this? Why do you keep loving the both of us and going back to her?" I looked at Cecelia and the honest answer to that question was that I loved Shanice. I realized when I hurt her that my love for Cecelia was the friend type of love, she was my girl, we could kick it, but I never should have made her my wife. "I don't love the both of you, I love you," I told another lie. "It's just, coming back here and seeing she never moved any of her things out, just brought back a lot of memories. I got caught up in memories, sweetheart. But that's no excuse for the way I've treated you." A smile formed across her face and I knew I'd done just what my mother demanded I do and as happy as that made Cecelia, it hurt me. I felt I deserved to be happy. I deserved to fix what I'd broken with Shanice.

Chapter 6

MAXWELL

I pulled out the bottle of Crown I kept in the bottom drawer of my desk and took a long drink from it. Handling this situation with Shanice had been harder than I wanted to admit and I needed some type of escape. "I saw that, what's going on man?" First Sergeant Jackson walked into my office and shut the door behind him. He'd become a great friend and confidant since I'd taken over as the company commander of Alpha Company. "Nothing, Jackson." I shook my head and placed the bottle back in the drawer. "It has to be something. You're sitting in your office with the door wide open, drinking. Picture if somcone other than me would have seen that. What if one of these soldiers would have seen it and reported it to IG?

Talk to me, bro, not as your co-worker, but as your friend. What's going on?" I sighed and lowered my head. I knew this was what the Army was all about. Soldiers helping each other when they needed it, talking to someone when you were feeling down so you wouldn't make the wrong choices. I preached that to my company every day and here I was drinking instead of talking. "It's Shanice. I don't think I'm ever getting her back. She has a crazy ass sister she just found out about who claims she's pregnant by me, but I never even slept with crazy, and there was no protection used the last time I slept with Shanice, so I'm sure she could possibly be pregnant—" He cut me off. "She could? I thought you were a Christian and all that jazz." "I am, but I broke my vow of celibacy when I got with Shanice because I just knew she was going to be my wife." I shook my head. "Well you know I'm not into all of that God stuff, so I don't know what to say other than maybe you should have still waited if you felt like God brought her to you." Jackson made a lot of sense and I definitely wasn't thinking like that. I'd been so happy to have Shanice in my life I had thrown caution to the wind and had started living like we'd already taken those vows. "You're right man, now I feel real lost." I took the bottle back out and offered him some. "No, and you shouldn't either. We're on duty, not to mention you have a formation at 1330." "Yeah, you're right." I took another sip as if he hadn't said a word. It was about six-thirty and I was just leaving my office. I decided to stay for a while because, after formation, I'd sat in my office drinking like I was at the bar and I didn't need anyone seeing me leave drunk. I made my way to my car and felt like I was okay to drive. I'd normally call a cab, but I knew I was good enough to make it home. "All, on me I don't deserve it She's just a little too perfect She's just a little too worth it I don't deserve her at all, no not at all I only text her, man I never call I'm still a canine at heart, I'm a dog" I turned Drake's song "Company", all the way up, testing out my Beats by Dre car speakers and they were flawless. The way it beat in the trunk and didn't sound distorted let me know I'd made a great investment. I made my way off post, headed toward my mother's house. Traffic was flowing smoothly as I got over into the far left lane singing along with Drake like I was featured on the album. I called my mom to make sure she was home and as soon as I hung up the call I saw red and blue flashing lights behind me. I pulled my car over and prayed they'd go around me but, just my luck, he was pulling me over. "Damn! Act natural, Max," I said out loud as the officer got of the car.

Chapter 7
SHANICE

I sat outside my grandmother's house, trying to mentally prepare myself for the conversation we were about to have. Like Dan's mom, my grandma could be very sarcastic and patronizing when a topic came up she didn't want to discuss and I had a feeling this would be one of those times. She was a good woman, and she felt all the good she'd done in her life had reserved her a special seat next to Jesus in heaven, but after finding out about Sharon, I wondered about the bad choices my grandmother may have made. Maybe her seat next Jesus wasn't so secure. I hoped my grandmother had a good reason why she hadn't taken Sharon in. She was a foster mother for years until she chose to raise me and Tameka, so if she could take in all of those random kids, why not her own grandchild? Maybe, just maybe, Sharon was my father's child and my grandmother never knew anything about her. "Grams?" I called out when I noticed she wasn't in her usual seat in front the TV. "Stop yelling girl, I'm in the bathroom. Can I pee?" "My bad," I said under my breath. My grandmother came out of the bathroom and gestured for me to follow her into the kitchen. I knew she'd been baking because I could smell it from the doorway when I walked in. My grandmother stayed in a small three bedroom, one and a half bathroom house on Green Street. She'd been living there longer than I could remember and, when Dan offered to buy her a new house, she'd declined, stating she loved her home and would never leave it. "I haven't seen you or your sister in a while, what brings you by? Hopefully it ain't about no money because I don't have any." She always thought something was about money and always made it a point to say she was broke, and she knew she was lying. "Grams, when was the last time I asked you for money?" "Well, Tameka came begging a couple weeks ago, so I figured that boy you was with cut y'all off. That's why I never wanted to meet him or his little uppity family. I told you messing with Harris' was a bad idea. I know his daddy's family." She gave me a speech she'd been giving me since high school. She never liked Dan or his family, even though she'd never met them. She worked for Dan's grandfather years ago cleaning their house and she saw a lot of illegal activity that had taken place to get his grandfather where he was. And once he fired her because she wouldn't sleep with him, she hated their whole family no matter what generation it was. I'd tried for years to convince her to meet them and she never would, so Dan would periodically send money to her through me, but that was as far as my grandmother's relationship with the Harris family went. "Nobody cut me off, Grandma, but I told you we did end things." "Oh yeah, so he could marry that little foreign white girl." She tried to recall the conversation. "Something like that, but that's not why I'm here. I'm here because I need you to tell me what you know about me and Tameka having a sister named Sharon." My grandmother could barely look at me when I spoke Sharon's name and I knew she knew something. "Do you want a piece of this pound cake?" "No, I want to know what you know." "Find your mama, and talk to her," she snapped at me. I got loud with my grandma for the first time in my life. "No, Grandma, I'm talking to you. I'm not about to go looking for no crackhead!" "You might want to lower your voice, child. Now, I will tell you about Sharon, but it ain't much." She walked back over to the table and sat down in front of me, looking like I'd just discovered the biggest secret known to man.

Chapter 8

BETTY MAE

24 Years Ago

"I'm not about to keep raising these babies, Melissa!" I yelled at my daughter who was pregnant again and strung out on drugs. "Well, I can't raise um, Mama, I don't have no money or no house." I looked down at the two-year-old little girl she'd already left me to raise, who held on to my pant leg. I'd stopped being a foster parent to take care of my granddaughter, Shanice, and hadn't regretted it at all until today. "Where is Harvey?" She gave me attitude. "I don't know." "Have you even told him about Shanice?" "He don't need to know." She sounded stupid. I knew I played a part in Harvey not knowing about Shanice, but I did it to protect my granddaughter. Melissa had fallen in love with this boy and he'd turned her on to the drugs. She was a smart girl who had a promising future and it was thrown away just that fast because of what she felt was love. When she became pregnant with Shanice, I sent her to Arizona to stay with my sister and get clean so my grandbaby wouldn't have that mess in her system at birth. I made her promise not to tell Harvey and she made good on that promise. She brought Shanice back and, the first thing she did was call that boy and ended up right back in those streets with him. "So can you help me again, Mama? Can you call Aunt Barbra Jean and see if she will help?" Melissa stood in front of me scratching her neck because she needed a fix and she looked as frail as a twig. "I will call her." A tear fell from my eyes, seeing my daughter like this. The very next day she was on her way to Arizona for the second time to get clean and give birth. I prayed this would be the last time and my daughter would stay on a good clean path. Nine months later she returned with identical twin girls, Sharon and Tameka. She told me she was going to find Harvey, resume their life together, and she didn't want the twins. She said she wanted to give me the chance to take them before she signed them over to the state. Harvey had no idea he'd had three children with Melissa, but from what I'd heard, he'd gotten himself clean because he felt like Melissa kept leaving because of their drug habits and his bad influence on her. "I'll take one of them," I told her. "No, you have to take them both. How can you just take one?" "I can't afford three children, Melissa! I will take one, and you do what you will with the other." It broke my heart to make that decision, but I knew what I could afford and I couldn't go broke trying to take care of three kids that didn't belong to me. Melissa handed Tameka over and stormed out of the house with Sharon in tow. Melissa didn't return home for about three weeks, but when she did, it was just her, no baby. She'd found Harvey and told him Sharon was his child and he told her he'd raise her to the best of his ability, but he no longer wanted anything to do with Melissa unless she planned to live a clean life with him. She declined, gave him the baby and found her way back to the streets. I didn't see or hear from my daughter for three years. She came home clean and with a job. She said she wanted to be in Shanice and Tameka's life and the two of them were so happy to be with their mother, up until Shanice was in the eighth grade. Melissa ran into some old friend who she'd never tell me about. All she told me was that they were close when she was about fourteen, and she was happy to reconnect. Not even four months later, my baby was back on drugs and back in the streets after so many years of being clean. I never did hear anything else about Harvey and Sharon, other than he'd moved to Greensboro, but I made sure to pray for them daily. (Present Day) I looked at my grandmother in disbelief. I'd never even known my mother had been on drugs since before I was in the eighth grade. I'd thought that was when it all started. I remembered my mother being to me what most fathers are to their children, a superhero. I almost couldn't speak, but then it registered. I grew up hating my father for never being there and he never even knew me and Tameka existed. "I can't believe the two of you." I scowled at my grandmother. "You've been lying to me for twenty-six years!" "I'm sorry, Shanice, but we did it to protect you!" "Protect me? From what? Knowing my father? Hell, my father seems like the only responsible adult in this whole scenario! And how'd Sharon find us? How does she even know about us if my father never knew anything?" I had so many questions. "I don't know, Shanice! I'm sorry if you don't understand why things happened the way they did, but that's what happened." "And who the hell was this friend my mother reconnected with? Who took my mother away from us?" Tears started to fall from my eyes. It seemed all I did was cry here lately. My mom reconnects with someone she knew when she was fourteen, and then all of a sudden she's back on drugs and I'm back at my grandma's. "I don't know, Shanice. Your mother was a grown woman and, even when she was little, she never really told me her business. She's always been quiet and has always kept things to herself." My grandmother tried to explain, but I really wasn't interested in anything she had to say and I was damn sure her seat next to Jesus was taken. I got up from the table and headed to the door. "I guess I will be looking for a crackhead," I said to myself.

Chapter 9

LA'DRAYSHA

"**A**pplebee's?" I questioned Tina as soon as I sat down across from her. I knew she didn't have as much money as I did, but I had no problem paying as long as we were eating at a more upscale restaurant. "What's wrong with Applebee's? They have the two for $20, and great drinks." She lifted her sangria in the air. "Whatever you say." I rolled my eyes. Tina and I had become fast friends when Dan and Max started hanging out in high school. She was always a real down-to-earth person and the only person I ever confided in about my past. She was great at minding her business, as well as keeping secrets when you made things her business. "Anyway, what did you want to meet here for?" I asked as I put my utensils in a glass of hot water. I refused to use them and not know if they were clean or not. "You're so sadiddy," she said with a laugh. "I wanted to meet up with you because we haven't really talked in months. Ever since you found out about Max and Shanice. Did you cut me off because of that?" I could tell she was confused. I threw my hand in the air to dismiss her comment. "No, girl! I invited you to the dinner party, even though it ended so abruptly and we didn't really have time to talk. But I could care less about Maxwell and Shanice. Hell, I'm okay as long as she's with anyone except my son." "If you could care less, why are you still plotting on that girl then? If I didn't know any better I'd say it was you who broke the two of them up." She looked me dead in my eyes to see if I'd show any indication that she was right. I knew Tina well enough to know she didn't play about Maxwell and, if she knew I was behind this whole thing with Sharon, she'd return to her ghetto roots real quick and it wouldn't be pretty, so I lied. "I had nothing to do with that. I have other plans for Shanice's family and I am not including Maxwell in this mess." "If you say so, but let me find out any different and there won't be anything anybody can do to keep me off your ass! I love you, but don't mess with my son while you're trying to hurt this family, which I still don't understand." She shook her head. I'd told Tina the story about how Shanice's grandmother wouldn't adopt me and allowed me to stay caught up in the system. Everything I'd gone through, from that point on, was Betty Mae's fault. So yes, I made it my mission to cause her family as much pain and misery as I could. We ordered our food and as much as I didn't want to eat at Applebee's, I knew Tina would complain as usual that I felt like I was so much better just because I was used to fine dining and not dining on a deal. "So, you're complaining we haven't talked. What's new in your life? I see that rock on your hand." I'd scoped out Tina's engagement ring the moment I sat down. I knew whoever she was engaged to had to be middle class because I needed a magnifying glass to see the diamond. It was cute, though. "Yes, girl! I'm getting married! Everything has happened so fast, I don't know if we're really ready, but I do know this man is amazing. I met him at church; he was one of our new deacons and his name is Rowland. He relocated back here from Georgia about three years ago, after his wife died." I was a little bit jealous. To see Tina find love after all these years, and know I'd been holding on to my kid's father for the money and never truly finding happiness, did something to me. "I'm happy for you, girl."

I forced a smile and then started thinking about my brothers, because something she said struck me. I'd been trying to find them for years with no luck. I took a sip of my top shelf Long Island as I silently asked God what I did to deserve all this pain and unhappiness I'd had to endure in my life. "La'Draysha?" Tina called my name, snapping me out of the trance I seemed to have fallen into. "Yeah, girl?" "Are you okay?" "I'm fine, I'm fine. I was just thinking. I need to start the search for my brothers again. I want to know why neither of them ever tried to find me." Here I was at fifty-five years of age, still carrying pain from fifty years ago. "I'm sorry, girl. I couldn't imagine going all these years and not knowing the only family I have." "They're not my only family. I have Dan, Carla, and Danae." I made reference to my children. "You know what I mean." She rolled her eyes. I loved Tina. She was probably the only person in the world who loved me, other than my children. She had to love me, knowing all the evil thoughts I had toward Shanice and not share them with Maxwell. No friend could be truer than she was. We continued our meal and changed the subject so we could get some laughs and not be so serious.

Chapter 10

MAXWELL

"Thanks, man." I grabbed my stuff as Rowland and I walked out of the police station. They'd put me in a holding cell until he was able to come down and get me. I was glad I could call him and didn't have to call anyone from work, but I did know that I'd be standing in front of the Brigade Sergeant Major explaining myself and trying to convince him not to take my position away from me because of the DUI I'd just gotten. "No problem! I know you didn't want to involve your mother, plus she's out with one of her friends right now and this may have ruined her night." He stopped in front of me and gave me the once over. "I know I'm not your dad, but I'd like to think we've gotten close enough

41

for me to ask. What were you thinking, Max?" I lowered my head in shame. "I wasn't, man." "You're a real smart guy; whatever you're going through isn't worth your life or anyone else's." He gave sound advice and I listened. I didn't have it in me to disrespect the person who'd just bailed me out of jail just because he wasn't my dad. We walked outside to Rowland's 2012 Dodge Ram pick-up truck. It was one of the nicest trucks I'd seen, especially for an old dude. It was red with black twenty-four inch rims and the tint was as dark as the law would allow. He kept it clean and, as I got inside, I noticed he was just a clean dude, the interior was spotless. Truck looked like it belonged on the showroom floor. "We'll pick your car up in the morning, they've already towed it off the highway," he informed me. I nodded and he turned up the radio to drown out the silence. I began to sing along with the Isley Brothers. "Driftin' on a memory, Ain't no place I'd rather be, Than with you, yeah, Lovin' you, well, well, well." I looked out of the window and thought about Shanice and how I wanted to be living for her love. Rowland dropped me off at home and I almost didn't want to get out of the truck when I saw Sharon sitting on my porch. It was a little after midnight and, though I'd sobered up for the most part, I didn't have time for her foolishness. "What do you want?" I asked, standing in front of the door but not opening it. "You changed your locks." "Yes, crazy, I did. Now what?" "I don't know why you keep treating me like this, Max! We're about to have a baby. I'm Shanice's sister so you'll never be with her. Why can't we just start building our family?" "You're deranged! We aren't having a baby. You need to find your baby daddy because I'm not him!" "Maxwell! You'll see when I give birth and you get tested!" "I will gladly get tested because there is no way possible you're having my child. Now please get your crazy ass off my porch before I call the police." I took out my phone to let her know this time wasn't just a threat. She'd continued to violate the restraining order I had against her and I was finally sick of it. "Okay, I'll leave." She put her hands up in surrender and walked to her car. I shook my head. I couldn't believe I'd actually considered being her man at one point.

Chapter 11

DANDRIDGE

I dimmed the lights in the room of my penthouse suite. I had to make the night as special as possible for the woman I loved; there was no room for error. I had lit so many candles, I just knew the fire alarm was going to go off, but it didn't. Tonight would be unforgettable, not only because I was sharing it with my lady, but because I wasn't the most romantic guy in the world. I'd ordered room service and set the table. Red and pink rose petals were everywhere and I'd ordered all kinds of massage oils. I was going all in. I reached over for my iPod and turned on a mix I'd just recently made with all the best love songs I could think of. Making the mix was kind of hard because I was never really an R&B type of guy and normally I would have called Maxwell and asked him what songs would be good. But I had to get use to the fact it was just me, I no longer had a best friend. "When I feel what I feel Sometimes it's hard to tell you so You may not be in the mood to learn what you think you know" Aaliyah sang "At Your Best" softly through the speakers as my princess walked into the room looking around in complete shock, but with a smile on her face. "Wow, Dan! You did all of this for me?" "I told you, you deserve the world and I want to give it you." I pulled her close to me and kissed her with as much passion as I could muster. I wanted her to know exactly where my heart was. I wanted to sit down and eat first, but the sweet taste of her lip gloss on my lips made me want her more than I ever had. I held her close to me and backed her up to the bed as the music continued to play. The beauty of Aaliyah's voice in the song set the mood so perfectly – I knew she wouldn't be able to resist me. I laid her back on the bed and began kissing her. I allowed my hands to explore and undress her as I deepened our kiss. Our chemistry seemingly flawless, she lifted my shirt over my head, exposing my perfect body – a body I worked on daily and that's when the song changed to Usher's "Lay You Down". I took her succulent breasts into my mouth one at a time as I teased her middle with my fingers. Her reaction made me harder and harder. As much as I wanted to dive straight in, I knew I had to make love to her like she was the last woman on earth. I placed soft wet kisses on her stomach until I reached her love and paused. I looked up at her, praying she'd give me the go ahead. "Do it," she whispered. I stuck my tongue inside her and her juices were the sweetest I'd ever tasted. This woman had no idea the goodness she'd held back for so long. She moved her hips as I licked from the bottom to the top, stopping at her clit and gently sucking on it. She held onto my head for dear life as she experienced the first of many orgasms I'd planned to provide her with that night. "I need to feel you," she moaned. I pulled the condom out of my pocket and took off my jeans. I entered her slowly, being careful not to go all the way in too fast; I wanted her to feel me inch by inch. She threw her head back in pleasure as I worked her slow and deep. Beyonce's "Rocket" began to blare through the speakers and she surprised me. "Let me get on top." I obliged and flipped us over without having to pull myself out of her. She rocked her hips to the beat and I almost couldn't take it. She began to grind hard and that's when she reached her peak and gave way to another orgasm of her own. I'd promised myself I wouldn't cum until she'd gotten at least three, but the way she rode me, I couldn't hold true to that promise. She tightened her muscles around my shaft and rocked back, then forward, I held on to her hips and exploded into the condom. "Oh my God, girl!" I closed my eyes and tried to remember a time when it was ever that good. She hadn't said a word and I hoped she didn't regret it. "Shanice, baby, you okay?" I asked. "Yeah, I'm fine. Let's just shower and eat." "You want to shower together?" She never liked showering together before. "If you want to, if not I'm going first." She laughed. "No, together is cool." I got up and followed her into the bathroom. I knew this night would be amazing and I knew there was no way I could lose her again after this.

Chapter 12

SHANICE

I sat in my living room with the TV on, but not paying it any attention. I tried to process my entire week and nothing was making sense. I was envious of Sharon because I'd grown up all these years thinking my father didn't care about me and Tameka, when really he just didn't know. She got to spend her entire life with him and, from her level of success in the real estate business, I felt like he'd done something right. I loved my grandmother, but her and my mother had lied to us all these years. I couldn't wait for Tameka to finally get to my house so I could tell her everything our grandmother had told me about our mother, plus I had a feeling Tameka knew exactly where I could find Melissa. "You okay?" Dan asked, walking into the living room with a towel wrapped around his waist, but still dripping wet from his shower. He'd spent the last few nights at my place and I wondered what lies he'd told Cecelia. "No, not really. You should go. I don't want you to stay here tonight." I spoke honestly and I could tell he wasn't happy with what I was saying. "I'm good here." "I know you're good, but I would like for you to leave. I appreciate your company, but I'd like to talk to my sister privately, and—" He cut me off. "And you don't want her to know I've been here. I get it." He'd been a good friend and for the moment he was taking care of my needs, but I knew he thought what we were doing was more than a friends-with-benefits type situation, when it wasn't. It was just convenient for me. Dan had no idea how much his lies hurt me, changed me even, there was no way I could take him seriously, not now at least. "Thanks for understanding!" I flashed him a half smile. "Yeah." He'd walked back in the room to get dressed when I heard a knock on my door. I knew it couldn't have been Tameka because when I'd spoken to her a little over twenty minutes ago, she said she was just getting on the highway. "Who is it?" I called out, because for some reason I couldn't see anyone through the peephole. The person knocked again. "Who is it?" Again they knocked. I looked through the peephole and was staring at an empty hall. I opened the door so I could look around and see if I saw anyone walking away, and that's when Maxwell stepped in front of the doorway, holding a beautiful bouquet of roses. "Max!" I hated that he kept popping up. I looked behind me and immediately felt like I'd just been caught cheating because Dan was making his way to the door. I looked up at Max and tried to apologize with my eyes. "Aren't you romantic," Dan said with a laugh as he approached us. "So this is why you've been treating me like shit." Max laughed slightly. "You deserve whatever you get." He threw the flowers at me and turned to walk away. "It's okay, bruh, you'll find someone." Dan laughed again and, before I knew it, Maxwell was all in Dan's face. "It's taking everything I have in me to be cool and not beat yo punkass. Don't say nothing, man. You're pretty much dead to me." Maxwell walked away and I could tell his words hurt Dan's feelings, even though he tried to pretend like it didn't faze him. "Are you okay?" I asked as I looked at the sad expression that had replaced his cockiness. "Yeah, I'm fine." "He's your best friend, Dan. I know you're not fine." I tried to get him to talk about it. "He was my best friend, until he messed around and fell in love with my woman. I'm going to go. I'll call you." He kissed me on my cheek and left. "Lord Jesus," I said out loud and shook my head as I closed the door behind him. I needed my sister and a very potent drink – our girls' night was definitely about to change to a girls' night out. "He did what?" Tameka was shocked Max had actually thrown the flowers at me. "Yes, honey! He was upset, but I could tell he was trying to control his anger as much as possible. I don't know what made him think it would be okay to just show up anyway." I took a shot the bartender called a Royal Fuck and scrunched up my face when it hit the back of my throat. "Big sis, you need to get it together! He showed up with flowers and you're complaining? And Dan? You're sleeping with Dan? Why? What good do you really think is going to come from you allowing him back into your life? I understand you're hurt that Max and Sharon are having a baby together, but you're not handling it right." She shook her head and drank the Porn Star shot she'd ordered. I sat there, thinking about what she said, but it felt so good to know I was using Dan just like he'd used me. Tameka was right about nothing good coming from it, but it felt good for the moment. I ordered another shot to prepare myself for the more serious conversation I needed to have with

Tameka about our grandmother holding the truth from us. She was definitely the more sensitive sister, so I hoped she took it all in without being too angry.

Chapter 13

LA'DRAYSHA

"We'll call you if we find anything, if not, we won't call." Dr. Freeburg gave me the no-news-is-good-news speech as we completed my mammogram. "Thank you, Doctor." He left the room so I could get dressed. I prayed they didn't find anything, considering I didn't even know my family history when it came to these kinds of things. I'd always just answered "no" to questions regarding family history because I'd assumed I came from a good healthy family, considering I never had any real health issues. For a fifty-five-year-old woman, I didn't look a day over thirty. I worked out with my personal trainer four times a week, and watched the things I ate for the most part, but doctor's offices still scared me up until I knew something. I looked down at my PalmPilot to see what else I had scheduled for today and I realized I'd forgotten all about my meeting with Sharon. I had a surefire plan that would get Maxwell to talk to her and take her back. Shanice would be devastated to know Max was back with Sharon, especially after all of the crazy things Sharon had done. "I'm so sorry I'm late. I had an appointment that went a little longer than I'd anticipated." "It's okay." Her voice was soft and sad. "What's the matter with you?" She lowered her head. "I don't want to do this anymore." "I paid you good money, Sharon; you will do as you're told." "No. I just want to have my baby. When Max takes the DNA test he'll know it's his. I can't believe I got myself caught up in this mess." She pulled an envelope out of her oversized purse and slid it across the table. "Here's the last two payments you made to me. I'm tired of everyone thinking I'm crazy, I'm not. You are." I cut my eyes at her. Sharon had no idea what I'd gone through to even find her. I'd known about her for years and, when Dan told me he was going house shopping with Max, I knew exactly who to send his way. The plan was perfect, but now Little Miss I'm Not Crazy wanted to get off track. "Listen little girl, you will keep this money. I've come up with a plan to get you and Max back together." "Who are you, Scarface? You can't force me to do what you say. I want to get to know my sisters. Shanice has done nothing to me and I've allowed you to pull me into the mess you and her have going on. I'm out." She grabbed her purse and stormed out of the restaurant. "Love overboard My love's in need help Love overboard I sure can't help myself" My phone started ringing and I couldn't help but wonder why Cecelia would be calling me, she should have been enjoying Dan and the fact they'd made up. "Hello." I answered in an unsure tone. "Hi, Miss Harris. Have you seen or heard from Dan?" "No. Why don't you know where your husband is?" I could tell she felt ashamed when it took her a moment to respond. "He told me he was coming to your house, but that was three days ago. I don't think he wants me here." I could hear the sadness in her voice. Cecelia had done nothing to deserve what my son was doing to her, not to mention she was six months pregnant with his baby. He did not need to be stressing her out. "Don't worry, Cecelia, he'll be home soon. Trust me." She hung up the phone without responding. I felt bad for her, but I knew that wherever Dan was, Shanice wasn't too far from him. I guessed everyone had lost their common sense by deciding they wanted to go against my demands. Sharon and Dan would get back on board or they'd soon regret making an enemy out of me.

Chapter 14

MAXWELL

First Sargent Jackson had just informed me he'd pulled some strings and talked to some of the right people to push my DUI under the rug. "Man, I really appreciate it." "It's no problem, just stay out from under the radar from here on out. There aren't too many more favors of this caliber I'll be able to ask." "It won't happen again. I don't know why I felt like driving was okay, I usually catch a cab when I'm drinking." "You're hurt, man, don't worry about it. Just don't do it again." It was odd having this conversation with him, considering he technically worked for me – but just as two grown men and friends, I knew he was right. I'd spent my weekend on the couch, pretty much staring into space. I couldn't believe Shanice had actually gone back to Dan. I'd done nothing to lose her and yet I was the one suffering. Dan, on the other hand, had done everything to lose her and he was reaping the benefits of Sharon's lies. I still didn't understand why she'd ruined my life like she had; people break up all the time. Had she gone this crazy on every nigga she came in contact with? I decided to get online and do a little research on Sharon, hoping she was who she said she was so it would be easier to find things out. I typed her name in the search bar and the only thing that popped up was a link to her Facebook page and the page of the real estate agency she worked for. I clicked on the real estate page and started clicking through the pictures and was shocked at what I found. I clicked on one particular picture, so I could see the date it was posted. "Year before last," I said aloud. I immediately pulled out my phone and logged into Facebook from the app so I could screenshot what I'd found. Things were starting to make a little bit of sense.

Chapter 15

DANDRIDGE

"**D**addy!" Danny ran up to me giving me a big hug. I hadn't been home in a few days and I knew I was going to end up arguin0g with Cecelia about it. "Hey, baby girl!" I picked her up and kissed her on her cheek. She immediately started talking my ear off about a show she'd been watching called Sofia the First. I listened to her and made sure to ask questions so she'd know Daddy was interested in everything she had to say. I knew I wasn't the best man in the world, but I did want to do everything in my power to show my daughter what a man should be in her life. Even though my father turned out to be gay, he raised me to be a better man than I was. I'd just chosen differently. "Dan, baby, can I talk to you please?" Cecelia emerged from the bedroom. "Can it wait? I haven't seen my little princess in a few days." I grabbed Danny and started tickling her. "I'm going to take you to Chuck-E-Cheese!" I said in my most excited tone. They didn't have a Chuck-E-Cheese in Spain and I knew she'd have a ball, and I also knew it would get me out of talking to Cecelia. "You haven't seen your wife in a few days either! Why did you apologize if you were just going to go back to her again?" "I didn't go back to her. I was at a friend's," I lied. "What friend, Dan? You were not with Maxwell because you two are not friends anymore and he is the only friend I have ever heard you talk about." "Well, I have other friends. Can you please stop grilling me? I wasn't with her!" I was starting to get angry. Cecelia was right, but I hated accusations without proof. "You are such a liar," she said, walking away shaking her head. I knew I was hurting her and, even though I wanted to care, I didn't because the only thing keeping us together was my mother.

Chapter 16

SHANICE

really needed someone to talk to, so I texted Dan. "Can you meet me at the track?" Dan always had a way of being there for me like no one else could, which is why I hated so much that he'd destroyed all we'd built together. I'd endured all the bullshit, just to be left alone, wishing things would have turned out differently. Had he done right, I never would have fell for Maxwell and I wouldn't be hurting inside the way I was. I cared for Dan, but I didn't love him. I loved Max, but it was impossible for us to be together, so giving him the cold shoulder was the only way I knew how to handle the situation. I'd been calling Sharon but she'd been sending me to voicemail and I couldn't get in touch with Tameka either. After telling her everything our grandmother told me, she was just as hurt, if not more, than I was. Neither of us could believe our grandmother would keep something that big from us for all these years. Tameka wanted a father to be her Superman in life way more than I did. Maybe that's why she had three kids and three baby daddies. My little sister had daddy issues and, because all of them were much older than us, she kept trying to find one in these men. He texted back and reality hit me again. "Sorry. Me and my family are out. Later?" Dan couldn't put me first because he had two other women in his life who came before me. "Don't worry about it, I'll just call someone else." "Max?" "Why does it have to be Max? It's not you, so don't worry about it." "Ok Shanice. If you want to be mad that's on you. I'll talk to you later." I hated arguing through text messaging, but I had to admit it did piss me off he'd just put me on the back burner and, as always, wasn't thinking of anyone but himself. I was not about to wait around for him to meet me. I got in my car and headed back to Cary. "Hey, Christine, do you need any help tonight?" I called my employer to see if she wanted me to come in. She'd been very understanding over the past week to my situation when I told her I was going through some family stuff and I'd just found out I had a sister we never even knew existed. But going home and being alone just wasn't what I felt like doing, so if she needed me at work, I could at least do that to keep my mind off of things. "No, we have it pretty much taken care of. But if you want to come in, I don't see a problem." "Okay. I'll be there in thirty." I hung up the phone and made a detour toward my job instead of my condo. I still couldn't believe Dan had blown me off the way he had, but it was cool. I knew exactly where he'd be later. I shook my head at the thought. I had no idea how I went from being his woman to being the side chick.

Chapter 17

MAXWELL

I walked into my mother's house and took a deep breath before I went into the living room. I knew it was Thursday and my mother was going to be a little peeved I'd interrupted her Shonda shows, but this was important. "Hey, Ma! Which show you watching right now?" I asked. Her eyes glued to the TV like it would be the end of the world if she missed something. "Grey's! So if you coming in here, you gon' have to be quiet until How to Get Away With Murder goes off." "Ma, I'm not about to sit here being quiet until 11:00." She had lost her mind if she thought I'd come over there to watch those shows with her. I did enjoy Scandal, but I wasn't too interested in the other two. "You have DVR record that stuff, I have something really important to show you." "What is it, Maxwell?" I sat down beside her and pulled out my phone, so I could pull up the picture I'd found on the real estate page. "Does this not strike you as odd?" She looked at the picture and shrugged. "So La'Draysha went to a real estate function and took a picture with Sharon." "Look at the date, Ma." She took the phone out of my hand and looked at the date on the picture. "No, this can't be right." "This picture was posted two years ago. Sharon told me she'd met Dan's mom a month before she became my realtor." I recalled a conversation between Sharon and me when we were almost a couple. "Something isn't right. Is there any way you can send this picture to me?" "Yeah, Ma, I can send it." "Okay, good. I'm about to call Draysha and see what's really going on." My mother had a look on her face I'd seen plenty of times. I hoped Dan's mom had a good reason for lying, because if she didn't, I knew my mother wouldn't take it lightly. My phone started going off with Sharon's ringtone, but this time it was a text. "Can you meet me somewhere to talk? No craziness, it's important." She couldn't have messaged me at a better time. I responded, "Yeah. I'll text later when and where." I would meet up with Sharon, but on my terms and in my own time. I knew my mother would get whatever answers she could from Dan's conniving mother and hopefully Sharon would help me understand what was going on.

Chapter 18

LA'DRAYSHA

41 Years Ago

"**S**top!" I yelled as I tried to squirm out from under him. He reeked of alcohol and his breath smelled like sour milk and whisky. "Shut up!" my adopted mother yelled as she watched and used her camcorder to record. This was a reoccurring thing they did to me and I hated them. I had plans to runaway soon, but I needed a little money. I saved my lunch money every week and was getting real close to my goal, but until then I had to endure the cruelty of these people and I blamed Miss Betty Mae. If she'd have fought for me, I would never be in this situation. I began to scream as loud as I could while twisting and turning. I couldn't take it anymore. "Tape her mouth, honey," Jim Bo instructed her. She sat the camcorder down just long enough to do as she was told. He held my arms and used his knees to spread my legs to allow himself access to me. Tears started to flow from my eyes, wondering why they continued to do this to me. When I first moved in with Jim Bo and Kat, they seemed to be the sweetest people you'd ever met. They had a real nice two-story Victorian home and both worked good jobs. Jim Bo owned his own towing company and Kat owned a retail store in downtown Raleigh. They gave me nice things, things I've never had, I thought they were the best parents I could have gotten placed with permanently. After about four months of being in their home, things started to change and they would make comments about how beautiful they thought I was and they could do something with me. It freaked me out, but I thought they were just complimenting me until the rapes started. The first time it happened, Jim Bo came into my room drunk and started feeling on me in ways no one ever had. It scared me because I knew it was wrong and he was a fat, hillbilly looking man. Yes, he was cleaned up, but you could tell he grew up in somebody's trailer park. He stuck his fingers in my vagina and I jumped back because it hurt and scared me. "Please stop," I said. "It's okay, girl. You're safe with us." I saw Kat standing in the corner with her camcorder ready to record whatever it was he'd planned to do. "Kiss me," Jim Bo said as he puckered up his lips and I could smell his nasty breath before he even leaned in. "No!" I immediately started to cry. I knew within myself what was about to happen to me, but I didn't want to believe these people, who were so nice not even five months ago, were about to do it. "Lay back, girl," Kat instructed. "No!" I yelled again. "Oh, you're going to lay back and you're going to like it." Jim Bo forced me on my back and began to tear at my clothes until my vagina was exposed. "You thought you were going to live here and not pay rent," he said while forcing himself inside me. I cried like I'd never cried before. It was my first time, and my virginity was being stolen from me. I was twelve years old. "I don't know why you're crying and trying to scream, little girl. I don't know why you still fight it. You know how your rent gets paid here," Jim Bo yelled, pumping in and out of me four times and he was done. They had no idea what I had in store for them and how soon it would happen. I was very close to my goal amount of money and I'd made a friend whose mother was very fond of me. They lived in the projects right around the corner from Miss Betty Mae and, even though the lifestyle Jim Bo and Kat provided was better, it wasn't worth what I had to go through. For two years I'd get raped once a week and they called it my rent. I hated them and hated Betty Mae for allowing me to be given to these pedophiles. It was the night before my fifteenth birthday and time for me to execute my plan because I knew Jim Bo would be home by eleven and headed straight for my room. He'd wake Kat and they'd say they wanted to give me my birthday present and what I would get was definitely not a present. When I got home from school, I poured gasoline on the steps in the back of the house. I also stashed my gloves and matches there because no one ever went back there. I knew my plan would work. As soon as Kat went to sleep, I would sneak in their bedroom, steal as many of the tapes as I could fit in my backpack and then sneak to the back and wait until I heard Jim Bo's truck. I would stay just long enough for him to get into the house and then light the match. If anyone ever questioned me, I would say I was at Nola's all night and if they didn't believe my story, I would show them the tapes. I stood in the backyard for a few minutes and watched as the house quickly began to burn from the rear forward. My room was so close to the back of the house that I just knew neither of them would make it out. I smiled because they deserved what they got. I hopped over the fence and headed toward Nola's. I was free and their fate was sealed. Revenge felt so good that I'd vowed to always make people pay for the bad things they did to me. I didn't want to be a killer, but knew I was smart enough to come up with other creative ways to get my own sweet justice. (Present Day) "Are you sure you want me to spy on your son? You can't just ask him what he's been up to?" "I have this money to pay you. Don't question me. Just do what I'm asking." Sometimes my private investigator, Jamie, asked too many questions. I used him quite often when I needed to know what people were up to. He and I dated in college before I met Dan Sr. He also tracked down Melissa for me years ago, and Sharon as well. He was very loyal. Maybe because he knew all the foul things I'd done to people and he still carried a love for me that surpassed any love anyone had ever had. Once I finished with the Fuller family, I planned to give Jamie another chance, a real chance. I was going to give up this love I had for revenge and finally be happy. But after all I'd been through, there was no way I could live my life without bringing them down. Miss Betty Mae thought they were better than everybody else. Too good to love anyone but her own long term, and kids like me had to suffer for her selfishness. I wondered how much she was going to like it when I turned Shanice and Tameka against her and made Shanice's life crumble as well. I knew Shanice was her favorite, Tameka was just there. But nothing would hurt a parent or grandparent more than to see their children hurt and crumbling.

Chapter 19

DANDRIDGE

"I can't buy your love, don't even wanna try Sometimes the truth won't make you happy So I'm not gonna lie But don't ever question that my heart beats only for you It beats only for you" I watched Shanice light up as we sat in the café' around the corner from her condo listening to Ashley Ado cover Emeli Sande's song, "My Kind of Love". I'd blown her off the other day when she wanted to meet up at the track and talk and I knew I had to make it up to her. I wanted her to understand that my daughter came first and it wasn't so much Cecelia. "How'd you even know about this place?" "I did my research! You know I'm always trying to find new ways to show you that I love you." She looked at me like she used to when I knew there was no doubt she was mine, except I could see the sadness in her eyes at the same time and I knew it was because of all the pain I'd caused her. I reached across the table and grabbed her hand. "Shanice, please tell me you know I love you." "Can we just enjoy the show?" she said softly and I turned my attention back to Ashley. I wanted to tell Shanice everything and finally be honest with her, but I didn't want those types of problems with my mother. "Am I dropping you off, or do I get to stay?" Shanice hadn't said much since I'd told her I loved her at the café and now that we were back at her place, I didn't want to just assume I'd get to stay. "Um. You can go. Can we do lunch tomorrow at my restaurant or do you have family plans?" I could tell it killed her to ask me that. "No, we can meet. I guess I'll just get a room out here so I don't have to drive back." "Okay." She sat in the car for a moment as if she were thinking of something to say. "Does your wife know where you are?" I dismissed her question. "She's fine." I didn't want to talk to Shanice about Cecelia, just like I didn't want Shanice to ever bring Max up to me. I wanted her and I needed her to want me, too, but I knew deep inside she loved Max and talking about Cecelia was not going to help me sway her back in my direction. She shook her head. "Okay, Dan. Goodnight." She leaned over and kissed my cheek softly. Shanice had given me the entire spill on all she was going through and it was hurting me because I knew the root of all of her problems was my mother and I couldn't tell her that.

Chapter 20

MAXWELL

I stood outside of Sharon's apartment complex a little hesitant about going in. I knew I was dealing with a crazy woman, but didn't know if this would be some type of set-up. I called inside and told her I'd be more comfortable if she just came down and sat in my car to talk to me. It was pretty late, but my unit was preparing for a field problem and my hours were up in the air. She came down looking beautiful, different, more calm than crazy, so I had a feeling the conversation would go well instead of left. She spoke softly as she settled into the passenger side of the car. "Hey."

"Hey. Look, you know I'm not a beat-around-the-bush kind of guy. How do you really know Dan's mom?" "What do you mean? I told you how I know her." I couldn't believe she was going try and play stupid, when she was the one who called me and asked to talk. Why ask to talk if you're going to come with lies? "Okay. Explain this." I passed her the picture from the real estate page and it seemed like all the color drained from her face. "I'm sorry. I can't do this. I can't keep lying to you." She started to cry and hadn't even said anything yet. "We met a couple of years ago. I was working out of Durham at the time because, as I told you, I graduated from NC Central. She told me she knew my sisters and I was floored because I never even knew I had sisters. She showed me a picture of Shanice and Tameka and, when I saw Tameka, I knew she was telling the truth. Not to mention Shanice is the spitting image of our father, Harvey, who raised me." I didn't say anything. I shook my head in total disbelief. She'd told me her father had run off, just like mine had. "I told her I wanted to get to know them, but she told me she'd get back to me on that. She came up with this plan for us to meet, but then her son told her you were looking to buy a house. She immediately connected me with the right people and that's how the real estate office ended up sending me your way. She'd been playing games for over a year and I figured if all I had to do was sell her son's best friend a house to finally meet my sisters, it would be easy. But La'Draysha has so many other messy plans. This is your baby, though." My jaw tightened at the mention of the child. "How do you figure that's my baby? Why are you still being crazy?" "I just know, okay, Max?" She got of the car and slammed the door. I'd gotten a little insight into what was going, but now I just needed to understand why. What had Shanice really done to Miss Harris?

Chapter 21

SHANICE

"You called us here for what?" I looked across the table at a glowing Sharon. She looked beautiful pregnant and I hated her. In the short time I was with Maxwell, I'd prayed I'd be the one glowing because I was having his baby. She'd called me and Tameka and asked if we could all meet up because she had some things to tell us and, apparently, those things had a lot to do with Dan's mom. "I wanted to apologize first." I rolled my eyes at her. "Give her a chance, Shannie, she is our sister," Tameka's gullible ass chimed in. "Whatever! That hasn't even been proven, what DNA test have you taken? Until there is one we don't even know who our father is!" I shot her a look. "It's true, Shanice. I've talked to our father and he's willing to get a DNA test done. He was happy to know I found you, he had no idea." She spoke softly as if she didn't know if it was okay for her to speak at all. "Look, I don't have much time. What's the apology for? You knew you were our sister this whole time and yet you continued to try and hurt me. You're having Max's baby – that's hurt enough, don't you want to stop?" I was tired of looking at her. "Look, Shannie—" "It's Shanice. You don't know me like that." "Okay. Look, Shanice, I'm very sorry! I'm not the person I've come across as. I wasn't raised to do the things I've done. It was all because I was promised a lot of things, but I didn't know those things would come at the expense of me hurting my family members. Hell, Miss Harris didn't even know you were going to run to Max when you and Dan broke up. You kind of just helped her out by doing that." I was so confused, but Sharon quickly made things clear to me. I paced back and forth in front of Miss Harris' house. This lady was about to explain to me why she wanted to make my life so miserable. To promise my sister for over year we'd meet and then turn around and use her against me. What the fuck was this lady's issue? It was time to put it all on the table. She couldn't keep interfering with my life. How could one bitter ass woman take two people away from me who I loved so much? "Were you ever going to knock?" She startled me out of my thoughts. "No need. You're outside." I decided to get smart instead of showing her I was caught off guard. "You here for a reason?" I looked at her and it was like you could see the evil bouncing all off of her. "Why won't you leave me alone?" I asked. "Am I standing at your doorstep right now?" She looked me up and down and laughed slightly. "You know what I mean. What did I ever do to you?" "Ask your grandmother, and get the hell off my property. I didn't invite you here." She slammed the door in my face and left me standing there looking confused. How was everything leading back to my grandmother? What other secrets was this lady holding on to? I was beginning to feel like I didn't know my grandmother at all.

Chapter 22

LA'DRAYSHA

"You still aren't going to thank me?" I sat across from Melissa who I'd found about two months ago, after which, I checked her into a rehabilitation center. Some of my plans were falling through the cracks, but some things were still on track. I needed Melissa to be clean when everything blew up in Betty Mae's face. She looked at me and laughed. "You're going to be in a world of hurt one day, Draysha. You reap what you sow," she said as she rocked back and forth in her seat. "Like your mother will reap what she's sown. I got raped because of that woman." My temper flared up before I'd realized it. "Did my mother rape you?" "She gave me away, she gave me to rapist." "So, after all these years, you're still holding onto that? It's not her fault your adoptive parents were sick. You want me to thank you? Thank you?" She began scratching her arm and shaking a little. I knew she was still trying to cope without drugs. "Look at my arms, Draysha! Look at them! From years of me shooting up! I probably should be dead and that's your fault!" I was stunned. "Excuse me?" "You think I don't know? I know when you pretended to be my friend all those years ago it was because you wanted my mother to be hurt. You drugged me knowing I'd been clean, knowing all I needed was a taste and I'd be gone all over again." We stared at each other and I started to laugh. "Yeah, well I didn't think it would take me coming back and putting you in rehab for you to get clean again. Just like your mother, you're weak. I can't wait to see your family crumble right before Betty Mae's eyes." I leaned in close to her so she'd hear the venom in my words. I signaled for one of the counselors as I got up to leave. "When I come back, you should thank me." The counselor approached and I gave my order to him. "My sister needs a little more time. No phone calls or visitors other than me. Some of the things she said disturbed me a little." "Yes ma'am." I'd paid off a few people to make sure Melissa had no outside contact. I didn't need her calling her family members and blowing up all I had in store.

Chapter 23

MAXWELL

"I got enemies, got a lot of enemies Got a lot of people tryna drain me of my energy They tryna take the wave from a nigga Fuckin' with the kid and pray for your nigga" I rode around town aimlessly, listening to the newest Drake album. I wanted to call Shanice, but knew there was no point in that. I'd done everything I could possibly do to get her back and she chose Dan, so I knew it was time for me to move on. I had yet to hear anything from my mom regarding this situation with Dan's mom and it was starting to make me anxious. This lady was out of her mind, legit crazy. She toyed with her son's life just to make his girlfriend miserable and I now understood why Dan's sisters barely had anything to do with the woman. I silently thanked God for blessing me with a mother who rode for me no matter what. I wasn't built to handle a mother who would turn against me or conspire against the woman I chose to love. If she was that concerned with Dan's love life, she needed to marry him. I laughed at the thought. "Hello," I answered my phone when my music was interrupted by its ringing. I normally ignored private calls, but with my unit in the field, I felt it would be best to answer. "Hello," I said again when the person didn't respond. "Max?" "What do you want, Sharon? And why are you calling private?" "Didn't think you would answer if you knew it was me." "Okay. Well, I'm on the phone, what's up?" "Look. I really like you, and I was thinking." She paused for a moment before she continued. "Maybe we can start over. I'm not really crazy, you know that now. And since we're going to have this child—" I cut her off. "See, that's what makes you crazy. All I really need you to do is get back on Shanice's good side and tell her it's cool with you if she gives me another chance. I get that the two of you are sisters, but that's not my kid and I love Shanice." I was borderline yelling. "Okay, Max. I'll leave you alone until I go into labor, but I won't tell Shanice anything." She hung up without another word. I could tell she was angry, but I didn't care. I was just ready for her to have that baby so I could move on with my life knowing she finally found out the truth, that she'd convinced herself of something impossible.

Chapter 24

DANDRIDGE

"I can smell that bitch on you, Dan!" Cecelia yelled. I rolled my eyes and walked in the kitchen to get myself a water. I'd spent the better part of my morning making love to and talking to Shanice. I drove back home because Cecelia texted me and told me Danielle missed me. Come to find out, Danielle wasn't even home. She was with my sister Carla. "What do you want from me?" I asked in an almost defeated tone. "I want you to be honest with me and just let me go if you don't want to be with me." "I'm here, right?" "You haven't been here in almost a week, Dan. What kind of question is that? I want to leave you so bad, but I love you and you don't even see it. I put up with your shit—" "She did, too! A lot more shit

88

than you've ever put up with. I don't want to leave you, Cecelia, but I can't lie anymore and say I can stay away from her, because I can't." "Let's go back to Spain." I looked at her like she'd lost her mind. I no longer had a job in Spain and law school started very soon. "You can go, but Danny stays," I said coldly. She began to cry like she always did and I decided I didn't have time for it. I pulled out my phone and called my sister. I wasn't about to play these games with Cecelia. I was going to go hang out with my daughter and big sister for a little while. "You know Mama is going to kill you when she finds out about you messing around with Shanice. She likes Cecelia; she isn't going to let you screw her over." My sister looked at me with concern, warning me as if I didn't know what I was dealing with, with our mother. "That's why she's not going to find out." "See, this right here. This is why I don't deal with her. She hasn't known my business since high school because the bitch is too controlling and calculating. I can't believe any of us came from her evil ass." "Hey, hey! She's our mother! As much as I hate what she's putting me through right now, I still can't listen to you talk about her like that." Carla rolled her eyes. "Whatever, little bro. There's a lot you don't know about that woman and, left up to her, you'll never find out." My sister had a faraway look in her eyes when she made that statement. I was starting to feel like out of all the people who knew my mother, I was the only one in the dark about who she really was. Here lately, she was starting to show me. "If it's so much I don't know and you do, why don't you tell me?" "Have you talked to Dad lately?" She acted like I hadn't said a thing. "So, you're just going to dismiss the conversation." "No. I'll talk to you later. I just don't want to say anything else about Danny's grandmother in front of her." I knew Carla was lying. She had no intentions of talking to me later, but I decided I'd just play her game. "Yeah. I talked to him. We're supposed to be doing lunch next week sometime. He's on vacation with his dude right now." I answered her question and left it at that as I watched her push Danny on the swing.

Chapter 25

LA'DRAYSHA

I sat quietly in the back of the church as I waited on Tina to finish up with choir practice. She told me she needed to see me about an important issue and she also thought it would be the perfect time for me to meet her new boyfriend. I looked around the building, feeling out of place. I hadn't been to church since I lived with Betty Mae. Hadn't even dropped by for a quick prayer. Tina always invited me and I would politely decline her offer. What had God ever really done for me? I'd lost my mother at five years old, had been given away time and time again, and even when I thought Betty Mae loved me, she gave me to the people who would rape me and make me feel worthless, and then I married a man who turned out to be gay. I shook my head at the thought of these people singing to a God who'd never done a thing for me. Where was my fairytale ending? Where was the love their so-called God had promised? These people were fools in my eyes. They finished up their song and Tina came down off the choir stand to greet me, but it didn't seem as warm as it normally did. I could always tell when something was wrong with my girl because she'd put a guard up until she got to the bottom of things. The little church hug with the pat on the back she gave me let me know that whatever her issue was, it was with me. "What's going on?" I was curious to know. "We'll talk, just not here. Let me get my purse and you can meet me outside." She turned to walk over to the pew she'd left her purse in. I walked outside and waited, looking at all the people who seemed to be so happy after they'd finished praising their God and preparing for Sunday morning service. "They're so fake," I said out loud, though I was talking to myself. Tina approached me and pulled me to the side. "Draysha, I know you can be a lying evil person and yet I continue to be your friend because I believe people can eventually change and see the light, but I told you not to bring my son into your mess." As she spoke, I grew confused. I knew sending Sharon to Maxwell's was going to hurt Shanice, but I didn't think Maxwell actually cared about the girl. I thought he and Dan were just passing her back and forth. "What are you talking about it?" I played dumb. "What is this?" She threw a picture at me and that's when I realized she really didn't know much at all. "Sharon and me. What does this picture have to do with Maxwell?" "You think I'm stupid, don't you? That girl didn't come into my son's life by accident. You set this up from the beginning. How did you even know Shanice would run to Max?" I looked at her through squinted eyes. "I had no idea Shanice would go to Maxwell. Max was never a part of my plans to get back at Shanice, and he still isn't." I was being truthful. Maxwell just happened to get caught in the crossfire when Sharon told me he'd dumped her for Shanice. Tameka had never told me anything about Shanice moving on, that was just the story I'd told. "My son loves Shanice and, because of you, he may never get to be with her again. I understand you want to make that family miserable, but now it's affecting my family. You need to let this go, you've been bitter for way too many years." Her tone was demanding and I didn't like it. "Everything was stolen from me, Tina! My mother, my brothers—" My sentence was interrupted when a tall handsome man walked up to Tina. "You ready, baby?" he asked. "Rowland," my voice was barely audible. I couldn't believe it was him.

Chapter 26

MAXWELL

"**D**amn, baby, you feel so good." I looked down into the eyes of the sexy caramel colored female I'd been eying at work for a while now. I knew I shouldn't have her in my home, and definitely not in bed, but I needed someone to take my mind off of Shanice and Dan. "Captain Taylor!" she called my name and that's when I realized I never even told the girl she could call me by my first name. "Harder!" she screamed. I was bit thrown off because I was used to really making love, but in this case we weren't in love, I was just using her. I thrust myself into her as hard as I could and put my hand on her throat. I made sure not to choke her too tight, but tight enough and I could tell she liked it. The look of pleasure that passed across her face made me drive myself as deep as I could possibly go. "Yeees, Daddy!" she whispered as I continued to pound myself in and out of her. I flipped her over and entered her from the back, mesmerized by the way her ass seemed to jiggle with each thrust. Gabriel had the biggest ass I'd ever seen and right now it was heaven. I slapped her ass and she yelled, "Yes, Daddy, do it again!" I immediately obliged. I grabbed her hair and rode her from behind as she looked back over her shoulder. This girl seemed to be competing with me and I was loving every minute of it. She bucked back and then did the unthinkable. She reached behind her and started massaging my balls as I went in hard and deep. "Oh shit!" Her hand on my balls took me there. I released all of my frustrations into the condom and collapsed beside her. I lay still for a while, looking up at the ceiling. I heard Gabriel say, "That was amazing." "Yeah, it was straight." She lifted up on her elbow and glared at me. "It was straight?" I could hear all the attitude jumping out the back of her throat. "You heard me." I got up out of the bed and went to flush the condom and hop in the shower. I'd never slept with a woman just to sleep with her; I'd always valued myself and women more than that. I looked at every woman like I'd want a man to look at my mother, like she was worth something. But this situation with Shanice brought out things in me I never even knew existed. I was making decisions I never would have made prior to things going south between me and her. "You're still here?" I walked into my bedroom with a towel wrapped around my waist and Gabriel was staring at me like she wanted to go for round two. "Yes." She smiled. "Well, it's getting pretty late. You should head back to post." I didn't want her to think I was into sleepovers. "I don't have a car." I lowered my head and started laughing. "I would get the girl with no car," I said under my breath. "Okay, well I'll call you a cab and pay your way back, but you can't stay here." "So you can have sex with me, but I can't stay? All y'all niggas are the same. It's cool, though." She started grabbing her clothes. "You can shower first if you want to." I shrugged and left her to do what she pleased. I just knew I was going to have to be nice to her from here on out because I'd just done some shit that could ruin my entire career.

Chapter 27

SHANICE

I sat in the lab where they were administering the DNA test for me and Tameka. Tameka was overly excited we may finally be meeting our father, considering we hadn't heard from our mother in a couple of months. The last time we'd heard from her, she was begging Tameka for money and it caused problems between us because I wasn't willing to contribute to her habit. I just prayed she was alright. I hadn't spoken to my grandmother in weeks because I was afraid of what she might say this time. I had no clue what her link to Dan's family was, but I knew if she was involved with Miss Harris, it wasn't good, and my grandmother was the last person I wanted to hate. "You alright?" Dan rubbed my back softly. He wanted to be there for me and here lately, he had. I felt bad for Cecelia, but then again I didn't. From what I understood, she knew about me the entire time her and Dan had been together, while I had been in the dark about her. I had to admit to myself that I wished Maxwell was standing beside me, but ever since the night he'd come by and saw Dan, he hadn't spoken two words to me and I knew he'd given up. I couldn't say I blamed him, but I really wished he hadn't. "The test is done. We'll contact you guys with the results as soon as we get Mr. Harvey Grant's results." Dr. Gilmore shook our hands and we all left. I was nervous and said a silent prayer that if this man was our father, then at least someone had told me the truth. It was just funny that "someone" had happened to be Sharon. "Oh, right there." I threw my head back on the arm of the couch as Dan massaged my feet. I'd been complaining all day about how much my feet had been hurting from standing so long at work. Dan hated feet, so I knew he was only massaging them because he wanted me to give him another chance at being my man. "You better be glad you have pretty well-kept feet," he joked. "I've always had pretty feet and you never touched them before." We both laughed. "Do you ever wonder if the rumors are true?" I turned the conversation to a serious one. "What rumors?" I paused for a moment because I knew what subjects were touchy for Dan. "Well, the DNA test today made me ask...the rumors about Dan Senior not being your father." Dan pushed my legs out of his lap and hesitated before answering. "Yes, I've wondered before. But at this point it doesn't matter if he is by blood or not. He still raised me and loved me as his, even when people swore my mother had stepped out him when she got pregnant. It doesn't help that I look just like my mom. But no matter what, he's my father." The look on his face told me he'd probably thought about it more than a few times and just never said anything. "Can I ask you something?" "You know you can ask me anything," I said. "Do you love Maxwell more than you do me?" His question caught me off guard, but as much as I didn't want to answer the question, I had to. "I love Maxwell in a totally different way than I do you. It's hard to compare by saying it's more or less." "If you say so." He pulled my legs back up into his lap and continued my foot massage. We didn't talk much for the rest of the time he was there. As always, he had to leave because he couldn't be away from his daughter for too long.

Chapter 28

DANDRIDGE

I looked around my mother's dining room. "What are we here for?" She'd called me and my sisters to the house for Sunday dinner, which we'd never had before. My mother was different in the way she loved, which was probably why I'd turned out to be so selfish. Changing that was hard. "I don't know, but I'm not staying long. She knows I don't fool with her." My oldest sister Danae rolled her eyes at me like I'd done something to her. Carla laughed and lightened the mood. "I'm just here for the food, really." "You're here because I need to talk to you." My mother walked in and started placing the store bought food on the table, trying to make it look like she'd really cooked something. "Well, can you start talking? I have plans." Danae hated my mother.

She always came over when it was something family related but, outside of that, we all barely saw her. "I just wanted to let you guys know I've made some changes to my will. I've split everything half and half." We all looked at her with confusion plastered to our faces. Carla was the first one to speak. "Half and half? You do know you have three children?" "Well, Danae has nothing to do with me and that's okay. We are both better off that way. And Carla, I know you don't too much like me, but you still respect me. And Dan. My baby boy. My defiant baby boy." I glared at her because I had no idea why she wanted to insult me. "Dan has listening problems. So, as of now, Dan gets nothing." I shook my head because my mother was doing the absolute most. "I see the smirk on your face, but I'm sure this will kill it. I still have power of attorney over your father's will as well." My sister's and I both looked shocked. Why would that man divorce and still allow her power of attorney to make changes to his will? He knew she was evil. "Why are you doing this?" Danae asked. "What has Dan done that's so wrong?" "He continues to pursue Shanice. I do remember not too long ago telling him to leave her alone. And I have someone here who needs to speak with you." Cecelia emerged from the kitchen and, at that point,

I didn't know what my mother was doing. "I listened to you. You told me to work my marriage out, that's what we've been doing." I lied and prayed Cecelia wouldn't say anything. "Liar," she spat at me and I knew everything was about to blow up. "After talking to me, Cecelia realized she's a broken woman, and even with your prenup, she can take you for pretty much everything you have." "You bitch!" I heard myself call my mother out of her name. "She can't take anything from me." I felt myself breathing harder than normal. "So you called everyone here to embarrass Dan? This is your son! Your baby, and you want to tear him down over some bullshit? I want no part in this. I'm leaving." Danae grabbed her purse and headed for the door. "Actually, son, that's where you're wrong. In your prenup it says you will leave the marriage with whatever you came in with and she will be awarded half of everything accumulated during the marriage. Is Shanice worth you losing half of everything you've earned in the past two years?" I was so angry I had half a mind to slap the spit out of my mother's mouth. "I'm not lying. I don't have anything to do with Shanice anymore." My mother let out a vicious laugh and threw down a manila envelope she'd been holding ever since she walked into the dining room. "Go ahead take a look." She smirked. I opened it up and almost fell over. There were very intimate pictures of myself and Shanice from the past few weeks. Photos of use having dinner, of our frequent visits to the café enjoying live music, and photos of me at her house. "The two of you had me followed?" "No, son, I had you followed. Apparently you'd been telling your wife to fuck off because you were going to be with that little whore who jumped on your best friend anyway." "She's not a whore." "Dandridge, you have to make a choice and make it now." I shook my head at the both of them. "I'll call you later Carla." I hugged my sister and headed for the door. I wasn't about to be backed into a corner. I had two months to make Shanice love me again, the way she had before. I had a gut feeling this whole situation surrounding Sharon was going to blow up in my face, all because I'd listened to my mother.

Chapter 29

MAXWELL

Gabriel was staring a hole through me as I called the company to attention. I'd been ignoring her phone calls all weekend, then sending short text telling her I'd get back to her because I was busy. She was a very beautiful girl, but not really my type and way too young. She'd just turned nineteen the week before I slept with her, and she was way too easy to get into bed. Most Army females were. I'd seen my co-workers pull too many girls and then kick them to the curb once they gave it up after date number two. "At ease!" I yelled. I needed to address my company and know I had their full attention. "It's Motor Monday and today's focus is tires. Tires, tires, tires! Check your tires and make sure they are fully mission-capable. You guys just came out of the field, so this week is solely dedicated to recovery, nothing is more important than making sure our equipment is good and ready for the next mission. So, with that being said, I'm going to fall you out and everybody get straight to work." I gave my spiel and released everyone to their sections to begin the recovery process. "Excuse me, Captain Taylor, may I speak to you?" I heard Gabriel's voice behind me. "In relation to?" I asked her. "Work." I laughed. "Yes, Private Moore, you can, after you use the proper channels." This girl was not about to treat me like I was her man over one night together. She knew there was a chain she had to go through before she could speak with me. "I wanted to use my open door policy." She tried it. "And that's fine, but have you informed your NCO that you need to skip everyone else and speak to me?" She smirked. "I'll do just that. Thanks, sir." "No problem, Private. Let's not make a habit of you approaching me with issues before speaking with your NCO." She turned to walk away and I exhaled. I knew I shouldn't have slept with that girl, but she was fine, damn fine, and I had to admit the sex wasn't too bad either. "May I come in?" I looked up and saw Gabriel standing in the doorway of my office. I'd gotten the call not too long after she'd said she wanted to use her open door policy and I purposely waited till the end of the day to give her that time. I had no idea where the talk was going to go. "Yes," I answered. "May I shut the door?" This girl was crazy. I never talked to any soldier with my door closed, but with her I figured it may be best, considering I didn't know exactly what she wanted with me. I opened up my voice memo app on my phone and pressed record just in case I needed it later and motioned for her to go ahead and shut the door. What caught me off guard was her actually locking it. I silently Thanked God that everyone in my office had already gone home because, had someone come jiggling that door knob, we'd be in quite the situation. "What do you need Private Moore?" I wanted to go ahead and get this girl out of my office. "You." Her tone was matter-of-fact. "Excuse me?" "I need you." She walked over to my desk and started massaging my shoulders. If I didn't know better, I would have sworn she was my woman. "I've been thinking about Friday night all weekend, and I need you." "Gabriel, we can't do this. Friday was a mistake." "Oh, was it?" She slowly trailed her hand down my top until she reached my lap. "Well, you may want to tell your other head it was a mistake." She laughed as her hand rested on my erection. I turned around to face her as I pushed her hand away. "You have to go." Women were way too bold these days, and I knew if she stayed any longer, it would not be good. "Stop trying to resist what we both know you want." She got on her knees in front of me and started unbuttoning my pants and, as much as I wanted to stop her, I couldn't. I was frozen. She pulled my rock hard penis out of my pants and took me into her warm mouth and began to sloppily suck it. I threw my head back. The girl was so good she had me biting my bottom lip. I placed my hands on the back of her head and pushed her mouth as far she'd allow me to, as she massaged the rest of my shaft with her hand. She licked and sucked on the head like it was the last lollipop she'd ever have and it sent waves through me I'd never felt. This girl was a pro at was she was doing. I felt myself on the brink of cumming, but I wasn't ready yet so I stopped her. "Take off your clothes!" I instructed and she did as she was told. I got up from the chair, retrieved a condom from my wallet, and bent her over my desk. I entered her from behind and watched as my balls slapped her ass with each thrust. She started to yell out and I immediately covered her mouth with my hand as I continued to ride her from behind. I felt her body almost give way and I knew she came. Now it was my turn. I increased my speed and removed my hand from her mouth as I held on to her hips and exploded inside the condom. She came looking for something and I gave it to her. We put our clothes back on and straightened everything back up. I reached for my phone and immediately deleted the recording from my voice memo. She glared at me. "Don't play games with me again." "Play games?" "Yes, that bullshit about using the chain to talk to you." I shook my head, I had no idea how I kept attracting crazy. "Hold on, Gabriel, what exactly do you think this is?" "I know what it is, but I also know what could happen to your career if anybody found out. So, like I said, do not play games with me again." She unlocked the door, and my knees almost buckled when I noticed Shanice and First Sergeant Jackson standing in the foyer. What was Shanice doing here?

Chapter 30

LA'DRAYSHA

I sat at the table across from Tina and Rowland, almost speechless. Out of all the bad that had happened in my life, I never would have thought a good thing would just walk up on me. "So how do you two know each other?" Tina was looking at me like I'd slept with her man. Rowland's eyes were glossy, as if he wanted to cry. "This is my older brother." I started to cry and so did he. It had been fifty years since I'd seen either of my brothers and, at sixty-two, my brother still looked as good as he had at twelve. "I can't believe it! I looked for you, and never could find you! I found Bobby. He's living in Florida and doing well," Rowland said, and I almost got upset. How was he able to find Bobby but not me? "You were in Georgia all this time?" I asked to take my mind away from the fact he and Bobby had been in contact for however many years. Tina just sat in her seat stunned. "Yeah. I got adopted not too long after they sent the three of us to separate foster families. The family that raised me were real good God-fearing people. They're no longer living now, though, which is why I decided to relocate back to North Carolina," he said. I rolled my eyes. "Wish I could say I'd been so lucky." I wanted to tell him right then and there all that I'd been through. Suffering through family after family until Betty Mae gave me to those evil people, then fending for myself from the age of fifteen. But I decided not to put all that on him, it wasn't his fault. "I'm calling Bobby right now." He pulled out his phone with so much excitement. Tina still hadn't said a word. Rowland passed me the phone after telling Bobby how we ran into each other in the church parking lot and tears streamed down my cheeks as I talked to him. We planned for him to visit in a couple weeks and, for the first time in years, I couldn't have been happier.

Chapter 31

DANDRIDGE

had been ignoring Shanice's phone calls ever since the meeting with my mother. I loved her, but I couldn't allow love to mess up all I'd worked for. In the last two years, I'd made over two million on my own, because I was smart enough to invest and I wasn't allowing Cecelia to walk away with money she didn't earn. My mother knew exactly what she was doing, and she also knew it would work. Cecelia had been walking on eggshells around me because she knew how pissed off I was that she was in cahoots with my mother. She was seven months pregnant and working my nerves, not to mention her and Sharon were due only a month apart. I prayed nobody questioned if that was Maxwell's child, but because I knew Max was never one to make dumb decisions, he'd be getting a DNA test just to prove to everyone he hadn't slept with Sharon like they thought. I was screwed either way. I needed to find a good attorney to figure out a way out of this marriage without having to pay. I called my sister Carla. It was time someone told me all the things they said I didn't know about my mother, because it was clear to me that she was never going to tell me. And Danae always shutdown whenever my mother came up in conversation. "This family is so screwed up," I said to myself as I listened to my sister's ringback tone – Mase ft. Total, "Tell Me What You Want". I shook my head. She was the only person I knew who still had a ringback. "What's up, baby bro?" She sounded real happy. "We need to talk. I want to know everything about our mother I don't know." I heard silence on the other end. I didn't know what could be so bad that Carla didn't want to talk to me about it. "You sure you want to have this conversation?" she finally asked. "Yeah, and don't tell me to meet you anywhere. Just tell me over the phone." "Okay." She sighed. "I don't know how true this is, but you already know people say dad isn't your real father. Well, apparently she cheated on him with a guy named Jamie back in the day. I've never seen him, but people say you favor him some." She started with public knowledge and I was almost irritated. "I don't want to know what I already know, Carla." "I know, boy, give me time. The reason why Danae doesn't like her is because she ruined one of her relationships, kind of like she did with you and Shanice, but it's deeper than what happened with you two. Apparently when he wouldn't leave Danae like mama demanded, the brakes in his car just mysteriously went out and, to this day, Danae thinks mama may not have done it, but she knows who did. That's why I encourage you to just let go of Shanice. She's a really sweet girl and I personally don't know what lengths mama will go to get rid of her. She's bitter, for whatever reason. I heard she had a hard life and I've heard her talking in her sleep about some woman named Betty Mae." As soon as I heard her say Betty Mae's name, I felt a pain in my stomach. It was Shanice's grandmother's name. What could my mom and Betty Mae have to do with each other? "What did you hear her say?" I had to know. "Nothing, really. She just kept screaming, 'this is all your fault, Betty Mae'." I closed my eyes and shook my head. Maybe my mother had nothing against Shanice at all, maybe it was her grandmother. But why mess with Shanice?

Chapter 32

SHANICE

"Your new conquest?" I asked as I stepped into Maxwell's office. I was jealous because the female who'd just walked out was absolutely gorgeous and I knew the look plastered across Maxwell's face. He'd just had sex with that girl. It was the same satisfying look he always wore after having sex with me. "What do you want, Shanice? Where's the love of your life?" I had to admit, he had every right to be upset. The reason I was there was because Dan wasn't answering my calls. I knew it made me look really bad and confused, but I wasn't. I knew from the first day I heard Maxwell say he loved me that I wanted him forever. But life got in the way and I needed someone. Dan was chosen as a placeholder –

not the love of my life. "Guess you've moved on." He laughed. "Did you come here for a reason? Last time I checked, I tried my damnedest to be with you and you chose Dan, so who I'm with or not with is definitely no business of yours." He was picking up his gym bag like he was just going to leave me in his office. I rolled my eyes and turned to walk away. "Okay." He stopped me. "So you didn't come here for a reason?" "I did, but now I see I shouldn't have come at all. I'm not about to kiss your ass because you're mad." "You should," he snapped. "So you're having a baby with my sister and you just expect me to accept that and move forward with you?" "I expect you to fucking believe me when I tell you the child is not mine! I expect the woman who says she loves me to do just that, love me! Stand by my side, be my rock, trust me because I haven't given you any reason not to. But I guess that's just too damn hard for your simpleminded damaged ass. Dan deserves you, because it is very clear he's the only man you can be that for, and you deserve whatever comes out of that bullshit!" he yelled and the sound of his voice felt like thunder. "I'm sorry, okay! Is that what you want to hear?" He shook his head. "You still don't get it, Shanice. It's not about what I want to hear." He brushed past and left me standing there. I'd actually come to his office to tell him I loved him and I was tired of playing these games and entertaining Dan's nonsense. It dawned on me how much I'd hurt him and the thought of him not ever forgiving me, hurt me to my core. I turned to leave and noticed Jackson standing right behind me. "Give it time. He still loves you." He winked and opened the door for me to leave. I hoped what he said was true.

Chapter 33

MAXWELL

It had been a few weeks since Shanice had come by my office. I'd been ignoring her ever since. I wanted her back, but I wasn't going to be anybody second choice. If she loved and wanted to be with me, Dan would have never come back into the picture. "You look so sexy," I told Gabriel as she modeled for me. She was wearing a lace red teddy she'd just recently purchased from Victoria's Secret. I'd continue to fool around with her just so she'd keep her mouth closed and because the sex was just so damn amazing. At first I thought it would help me get over all the bad that had taken place in my life. I quickly realized the more time I spent with her, she was beginning to fall for me and I personally could care less about her. She didn't possess the thing Sharon possessed that made me want her, and she was definitely not Shanice. She gleamed at the compliment. "Thank you, babe. I have something to show you!" "And what's that?" She lifted her teddy up and I noticed a tattoo on her stomach with my name on it. "Why do I keep getting these crazy girls?" I asked myself aloud. "Crazy?" She glared and I knew it was time to break things off with her. "Look. I can't keep doing this. You clearly feel some way about me that I do not feel about you." "So all these nights we spend together...you mean to tell me you don't like me?" I rubbed my forehead. I knew I could be putting myself in a bad position, but I had to be honest with her. "I like the sex, I don't like you, Gabriel. I don't even know you outside of the bedroom—" "Well, you can get to know me." She pouted and I started to feel bad. "That's the thing, I don't want to. You said you knew what this was, and now I see you don't. You need to get your clothes and go." "Maxwell, we can talk. I'm not a whore or a bad person. I'm sure you'll like me." Her age started to show as she begged. I shook my head. "I'm sorry, Gabriel." I walked over to the love seat where she'd put her bag with her clothes in it and handed it to her. "Get dressed. You need to go. And we don't need to continue this." She snatched her bag from me as tears filled her big brown eyes. "I know you're leaving me for the girl who came to work that day." "Does that even matter?" I asked. The look in her tear-filled eyes told me I'd truly broken her heart. I opened the door for her and she walked out without even changing back into her clothes. I was just glad she'd gotten a car so I wouldn't have to deal with her tears all the way back to post. "Get your shit together," I told myself.

Chapter 34

DANDRIDGE

I sat across from my father and the room was silent for a while. I wanted to know the truth once and for all. I'd made it a point not to speak to my mother about anything yet, but it didn't matter because she seemed to be distracted lately and, oddly enough, she seemed happy. I didn't want to ruin her mood, but I also wanted the evidence to back me up if I approached her with anything. This woman had had such a negative effect on my life in the past year and I kind of wanted to be the one to destroy her happiness. My dad finally broke the silence. "So what's going on, son? Is there a reason you asked me to come over?" "Look, I'm just going to be straight with you—" "Granddad!" My sentence was interrupted when Danny ran in the room to greet her grandfather. I loved seeing her with my family. Even my mother seemed to love her more than she did any of the rest of us. I looked back and saw Cecelia standing in the doorway, looking as sad as ever. I felt so bad hurting her the way that I was, but the fact was she and I should have never been together in the first place. She was a mistake that shouldn't have been made, a mistake that cost me everything I truly loved. "What were you saying?" my dad asked as he bounced Danny on his knee. I didn't believe in discussing certain things in front of children. "Danielle, go with your mother, baby, and let me and your grandfather talk." "Okay, Daddy!" She kissed him on his cheek and ran toward her mom. "Look, I just want the truth. Are you my father?" A sad expression passed across his face and I almost wanted to leave the room. "I don't know, son. I've never really cared to find out for sure. I've heard the rumors and whispers about your mother cheating on me and I know who with, but I've always loved you mine or not." I commended him on loving me, even while being unsure if I was really his son or not, but we needed to find out. If I wasn't his son, I'd have more than a few questions for my mother and this Jamie guy Carla seemed to think was my real father. I parked my car about a mile from Max's house. I really missed my boy and

I hated what we were going through because of a girl who loved us both, but I knew within myself she loved him more. I wanted to talk to him about the conversation I had with my dad, I wanted to hang out again, I wanted my brother back. I didn't know if Shanice had run to him again when I cut things off, which was why I was scared to just go over there. I didn't want another scene like the one at her house. It was like she'd been bouncing back and forth between the two of us, just looking for one of us to love her. And as much as I hated to admit it, Max was the better choice. I'd seen how he looked at her, had actually seen it for years and chose to ignore it because I knew she was mine and he'd never have her. Now that he had, I wondered if he'd get the fairytale ending with her I wanted so badly. I really just wanted to tell everybody the truth, expose my mother for the evil snake she was and let the chips fall where they may. I turned the key to restart the engine and turned Drake and Lil' Wayne up as they sang the "Brand New" remix. I didn't care if Shanice was there or not, Maxwell and I needed to talk.

Chapter 35

LA'DRAYSHA

"It's already done," the tall, bald dark-skinned convict told me with a straight face. "It wasn't supposed to be done until next week!" I yelled. I'd spent the past few nights at Tina's catching up with Rowland. We were both excited and awaiting the arrival of Bobby. Not too long before that, I'd paid this guy to do some dirty work for me – the last thing I needed done before I'd confront Betty Mae. I'd paid him to change Shanice's life forever, but I'd also given him a day to do it and he'd taken it upon himself to do it on his own time. "Yeah, well, I did it this week, Ma. So where is the rest of my money?" "I'm not giving you a dime. I called you here to call it off." "Well, you can't! I just said it's already done!

Now. Give me. My. Money!" He tried to use an intimidating tone with me. "Boy I'm not scared of you. I know yo mama and if she knew what you've done—" "I don't care, lady! Give me my money so we can be done with each other. You asked me to do something, I did it. Pay up." He pulled a gun from the small of his back and sat it on his lap just to let me know how serious he was about his money. I reached in my Louis Vuitton purse and handed him a brown paper bag that contained twenty-five thousand dollars, which was the final half I owed him for the job. "We don't know each other." I made it very clear to him that if Shanice went to the police and they found out who he was; I had nothing to do with it. I was not going to prison for anybody. He got out of my car and I drove away feeling bad about what I'd done. I never felt bad or had remorse for my actions before, but ever since I'd been reunited with my brothers, it seemed like everything had changed within a blink of an eye. Now that the deed was done, I knew I had to continue the path and the plan, no matter how happy I was or how bad I felt. Tina had warned me of karma if I decided to go through with everything, but it seemed to me that karma was on my side. I had my brothers back. Even though I was beginning to feel bad for the way I'd treated Shanice, all of my plans were seemingly going through even when people tried to throw me off course. If I had believed in God, I probably would have said he was good.

Chapter 36

SHANICE

got out of my car feeling exhausted. It was a packed night at Christine's and my feet were killing me. I just wanted to get in my bed and rest, considering I had the early shift in the morning. I hated when I worked nights and still had to be there again in early in the morning. I turned the lock to open the door and immediately froze. There was a man sitting on my couch and I had no idea who he was. My mind told me to run, but my feet wouldn't move. "What do you want? You can take anything, just don't hurt me," I heard myself say. He laughed and his stare never left mine. "That old lady was right, you're a gorgeous, little somebody! You know how long it's been since I had a sexy little mama like you?" He got up from my couch and started walking toward me and that's when my feet decided they could move. I turned to run out of the door, but he was quick and he grabbed me. He slammed the door before I could leave. "You're not going anywhere until the job is done." He pulled me close to his chest. "What job?" I yelled out of fear. "You're loud, I like um loud!" He took me over to the couch and laid me down while he continued to hold me. "Let me go!" "If you cooperate, I promise it won't hurt a bit." His voice was low and mean. "Please don't do this," I begged with tears rolling down my cheeks." "Shhhh, don't cry." He placed a finger over my lips and my skin crawled at his touch. "It'll be over soon." He ripped my leggings and quickly removed his pants, which were already unbuttoned and unzipped. I crossed my legs and he immediately placed his hand around my throat. "Open your fucking legs or I will choke you to death." He glared at me with dark eyes and his jaw clenched. I knew he wasn't kidding. "I'm trying to be nice to you, girl! I just came to do a job and leave. You want to let me do my job?" He taunted me like I was a child. He ran his hand down my inner thigh and touched me like I belonged to him. "This is going to be good." He put his finger in his mouth and smiled. He hovered over me and I trembled in fear. I never thought anything like this would happen to me. He forced himself inside of me as I cried, pleading with him to stop. I closed my eyes praying I'd wake up and discover this had all been a nightmare.

Chapter 37

MAXWELL

"**S**hanice, calm down! What's wrong?" I finally answered the phone after Shanice had called me at least twenty times back-to-back. She was crying hysterically and I couldn't make out what she was saying until it really hit me. "Max, I was raped." I finally heard her through her tears and my heart dropped to my feet. Who would do something so terrible to her? "Shanice, call the police. I'm on my way to you now!" I jumped out of bed and threw on some sweats and a t-shirt. I knew it was going to take me close to an hour and a half to get to her, but I couldn't let her go through this alone. I got in my car and said a prayer for God to heal and keep her because I knew after going through something like this, if she didn't lean on God, she would be a wreck. I also prayed and asked the Lord to help me not blame myself because all I could think about was if I had just talked to her the day she showed up at my job, we could have worked things out and she would have been with me...and safe. I pulled up to Shanice's and automatically got upset. There wasn't a police car in sight. She hadn't called and said anything about being in the hospital, so I knew she was just held up in her apartment, crying. I approached the door and saw it had been left cracked open. I pushed it and noticed nothing was out of place, except Shanice in the far corner of her living room in the fetal position, still crying. I ran over to her and wrapped my arms around her. She flinched, and pulled away. "Can you just sit here with me? Don't touch me, please." There was terror in her eyes and I began to cry with her. I couldn't picture her being scared of me. "I'm here, Shanice," I said as I just sat there with her. I wanted to beg her to go to the police, to tell someone other than me. But with my Army experience, I knew it was easier said than done. In most cases, women didn't tell. I just knew I'd have to make sure she didn't shower because if she decided in the morning she wanted to report it, they'd need the DNA.

Chapter 38

DANDRIDGE

Maxwell's car sped past me just as I turned on his street. I had no idea where he was going, but I knew he had to get there in a hurry. I tried to look inside to see if he had a passenger, but he was driving too fast. I hoped nothing had happened to his mother, because he was driving at emergency speed. In a way I was happy he was leaving. As much as I was ready to reunite and become boys again, I didn't know exactly what I was going to say or if he'd even be receptive. My mother sent me a text and I turned my car around. "Meet me at the house. I have some people I would like for you to meet." I really didn't want to see her, but I also didn't want to deal with the argument that would inevitably come if I said no. I walked into her house and saw two men sitting in the living room, laughing and talking to her. One I'd seen before – Max's soon-to-be stepdad and one I didn't recognize, but he and I favored each other. My mom was smiling like I'd never seen her smile before. It was genuine and seemed to be full of love. She normally looked the part of the evil bitch she was. "Is this my real father?" I started in on her before she had a chance to make introductions. I was angry! I couldn't believe she'd invite this man over here and not even give me a warning. "Your real father is Dandridge Senior! What's gotten in to you?" she yelled as I glared at her. If looks could have killed, I would have been motherless. "You think I believe you? You lie so effortlessly!" I turned to the man who was seemingly my twin. "Hi, Jamie! I'm your son, Dan the second. Sounds stupid, right?" I extended my hand to the man who looked clueless to what was going on around him. My mother walked up to me and slapped me so hard I swore spit fell from my mouth. But the look in her eyes told me the name Jamie did ring a bell for her. I wanted to slap her back so bad, but I knew it would be taking things too far, no matter how angry I was at her. But the more I looked at her, the more bitterness surfaced in my heart toward her because her whole existence seemed to revolve around ruining the lives of everyone she ever encountered. She'd shut out love on all levels and I knew eventually karma would bite her in the ass and I wanted to be around to see it. "These are my brothers, Bobby, and you've met Rowland before, he's dating Tina." I was confused. "Brothers?" "Yes!" She was back to that glowing smile she had when I first walked in. "You told me you were the only person left in your family after you lost your mother." I shook my head at her. "More lies, huh?" "No. We were all separated after our mother's death. I never even thought we'd see each other again." She smiled as she held onto Bobby's hand. "Has he met Carla and Danae?" "They're on the way over here. You just got here first." "Oh, okay. Well, it was nice meeting you, Bobby. Have my mother give you my number and we can catch up later. I just really don't want to be here." I dapped them both up and headed toward the door. Here she was fucking with everyone else's lives, but good things were happening for her. What kind of karma was that?

Chapter 39

SHANICE

Sat in the police station with Maxwell by my side. I didn't really want to file a report; I just wanted this to be over. Every time Max tried to take my hand or touch me in any kind of way, I'd flinch in pure terror and that, in itself, hurt me to my core. I just knew when Max came back into my life, if he came back into my life – all I'd want is to feel his touch. "Hi, are you Shanice Fuller?" A tall handsome cop came up to me, extending his hand. Maxwell shook his hand when he realized I wasn't going to. "Yes, sir, this is Shanice. She's a little rattled." He also answered for me. "Would you rather me go get my partner? She's a female. Detective Smith." I nodded and he turned to ask the receptionist to page Detective Smith. "It's going to get better, I promise." Maxwell tried to reassure me, but I just looked at him. I was grateful he was there for me and had even gotten emergency leave, but I just didn't look at him as Maxwell at the moment. He was just another man, another man who could potentially hurt me. Detective Smith joined us in the front and told me to follow her to a secluded room for questioning. She explained to Maxwell that he could stand at the window, but he couldn't be in the room. "So what happened last night, Miss Fuller?" Detective Smith jumped right in once we were both seated. I explained to her I'd come home to find this man sitting on my couch and that he had to have been sent by someone because he'd mentioned an old lady. I had a feeling of who the old lady was, but I couldn't believe Miss Harris had sent someone to actually do me bodily harm. How could I just say it was her when I didn't know for sure? Dan would never forgive me for that. I knew things were really over between he and I, a fact I didn't much care about, but I didn't want to mess up any chance we had of possibly being friends one day either. "I'm sorry you had to go through this, Miss Fuller, but I am going to tell you if you choose to move forward with this case, you will be questioned over and over again and have to relive the incident more times than you'd like. Are you prepared for that?" I nodded in response. "Okay, well, I'm going to call in our sketch artist and ask you to describe the man to him, and we can proceed from there." Again I nodded my agreement. A tall, lanky white guy walked in and I gave him a slight smile. He looked like the high school version of Maxwell, just white. "Hi, Miss Fuller. My name is Delmar. If you don't mind, will you describe for me the man who assaulted you?" "He was tall. Dark skin, like really dark. His eyes were dark brown, but cold, it was like his mission was to kill. He had really high cheek bones, and his lips were small. No offense, but more like white people lips, not full at all." "Do you remember the shape of his eyes, ma'am?" "They were like slanted almonds and his eyebrows were bushy, almost a unibrow." "Okay. That's all I need." I watched as he sketched away and the look on Detective Smith's face when he was done told me she knew this guy. "Are you sure you didn't miss any details?" she asked. "No, I didn't miss anything." I knew she could sense the attitude in my voice. Delmar turned the photo around and I almost jumped out of my seat at how good he'd drawn the man who had raped me. "That's him," I whispered. She shook her head. "His name is Frankie Curry. I can't believe he's done this again."

"Again!" I yelled. "Why is he wandering the streets if he's already a convicted rapist? I looked at the glass and could see the look of concern on Maxwell's face when he saw me stand up and yell at the detective. "It's not what you think, Miss Fuller. He was just released on good behavior a little over a month ago after serving twelve years for raping a teenage girl. He swore he was innocent and that she'd told him she was eighteen, but I guess old habits die hard. We'll start looking for him immediately." Tears started streaming from my eyes. I never understood why they released people who'd done such harm to others. I was all about second and sometimes third chances, but look at where this man's second chance had landed me. I was broken because of someone who could care less about other people, all because he knew how to act in prison.

Chapter 40

MAXWELL

I sat in the car with Shanice, listening to her tell me all about this guy Frankie Curry. I knew her feeling like he didn't deserve a second chance was justified, but for some reason none of this sat well with me. In my mind, Frankie was a victim as well. I had no doubt, after everything Sharon had told me about Dan's mom, she was the reason Shanice had been attacked. I just couldn't believe this man would get released from prison on good behavior and then turn around and do something he knew would land him right back there. I wanted to reach for Shanice's hand, but I knew she wouldn't allow me to touch her. I'd tired so many times and every time she looked horrified. "Out of all of the people you could have called, why did you call me?"

I had to know. "Because I love you, Max. I hate all of this stuff that has happened to keep us apart and I'm sorry for running to Dan instead of you the first time, even while you were trying so hard. It's just that the baby situation is hard to get over. And now," she paused, "now this." Her tears flowed heavily. "Look, I'm going to be with you the whole time. We're going to go inside the hospital so you can be examined and they can collect this man's DNA, and I'm not leaving your side after that. Shanice, you are my world, you always have been and I'm not letting you go over mistakes you've made or this situation. All I need is for you to believe me when I say this baby is not my baby. You know I'm a better man than that, I wouldn't deny a child I know I created." I looked her dead in her eyes so she'd know I wasn't lying to her, so she'd finally see the truth. "Okay," she said meekly and got out of the car so we could make our way into the hospital. It had been a long day but, I planned to make sure her days from this day forward would be nothing short of amazing. I pulled into my driveway, looked at a sleeping Shanice and smiled. I was happy she'd let me take care of her and be her knight. I needed her just as much as she needed me. I wanted to be angry with her for all the time she'd spent with Dan, and all the time she'd spent making sure we didn't work through things, but after all that had happened, I realized life was too short to walk around with an unforgiving heart. This woman was my dream and I loved her without condition, just as a man should love his wife. I had to make her my wife. But I knew I'd have to give her the time to heal.

Chapter 41

LA'DRAYSHA

I couldn't believe Dan had come in my house with such attitude and disrespect. "You told him?" I yelled at Dan Senior. "I didn't tell him anything," he said defensively. "Well, how the hell does he know about Jamie? Nobody knows other than you." "What's done in the dark, Draysha!" He got on my last damn nerve. The entire time we were married, Dan Senior knew about my love for Jamie and that I'd had an affair around the time I got pregnant with Dan. I'd always wondered why it had never bothered him up until the day I found out he himself had a secret. He never denied Dan or even asked me for a DNA test, he merely signed the birth certificate and loved Dan to no end. "You have some nerve to say that to me!" "Look, I can say this to you because you're not my wife anymore. You need to get over yourself and start treating people with more respect than you do. You sit there and you come up with the most elaborate plans to hurt those who don't do what you want them to do and eventually all your little secrets will come to light and I pray that God shows you mercy." "Oh, shut up! Aren't you a gay man? You better pray he shows you some of that same mercy!" I spat back at him. "Goodbye, Draysha! Don't call me again." He hung up before I could say anything. He told me not to call him, but I really needed to know how Dan knew about Jamie. I sent him a quick text because our conversation was far from over. "Call me when you stop acting like a female about things." I sat in my kitchen sipping on a glass of green tea and thinking about what had done to Shanice, and for the life of me I couldn't shake the guilty feeling I had. I never felt guilty for getting even. Maybe I felt that way because it was Betty Mae who I was really upset with and I knew I should have taken her out of here a long time ago. I should have done it after I'd run away from Kat and Billy. I knew it would hurt her to know Shanice had been raped but, Billy had stolen my innocence from me. And it was something Shanice had been able to give away of her own free will.

"Why am I second guessing myself?" I asked out loud, but knew I had no answers. Ever since my brothers had come back into my life, I was happy, and I genuinely wanted to take back all of the things I'd done to hurt people. I now realized I should have learned how to deal with those things instead of leaving a trail of pain in other people's lives, blaming them for my misfortune. Both of my brothers grew up with great God-fearing families, but here I was an atheist who played God for a living. "Snap out of it!" I shook my head trying to make sure I was seeing what I thought I was seeing. "Mama?" "Girl, all of those people deserved what you did to them. Your brothers are some punks. God? Do you think God would have let that woman kill me?" I shot to my feet and almost fell over a chair. I knew I was losing it. "Answer me, girl." "No, Mama, God wouldn't have done that." "Those people who died in the fire you started deserved it, baby. Don't let a little bit of happiness destroy you and make you feel bad for the things you've done." I smiled at my mother for giving me the confirmation I needed. Those people did indeed deserve that and so did Shanice. I couldn't wait to reunite the family with Melissa. Everything was going as planned. I smiled and my phone started to ring. It was my doctor I'd been avoiding for the past few weeks. I figured he was just trying to take me out on a date. He'd asked before and I'd declined, so there was no reason to entertain him by answering his calls now. He kept leaving me messages saying it was important I return his call, but I knew it was just so I'd call back. Men were simple like that.

Chapter 42

DANDRIDGE

I explained to Cecelia that it was over. "You're just going to have to take half of everything. I can't live like this anymore." I wanted nothing more than for her to stick around and follow her dreams, dreams she'd never see prosper in Spain, but I couldn't be her husband anymore. Hell, I wasn't much of a husband to her anyway. She deserved better and if her finding better meant her taking half of the things I'd earned since being with her, it was just a loss I was going to have to take. I loved my daughter and our unborn daughter, but I wasn't going to allow them to be raised by two unhappy parents. I'd been raised by two people who were living a lie and, even though I was spoiled, my mother wasn't the best at loving me because of her own bitterness and selfishness. I didn't want to be that parent to my kids, none of them. I still couldn't get over the fact Sharon would also be having my child soon. "Thanks for finally being honest." Cecelia had tears in her eyes, but I also saw a look of understanding. "Are you going to go back to her?" She asked a good question. It had been a few months since I'd spoken to Shannie and I didn't know if she was back with Maxwell or moved on to someone new. "I don't know if she'll even want me, but if she does, yes, I'll go back to her. I love you, Cecelia—" "But not like you love her." She finished my sentence for me. "Yeah." We sat in silence for a moment and, as much as I wanted to embrace her and apologize, I knew I shouldn't. I'd caused so much hell in both her and Shanice's life, I knew I was lucky Cecelia still loved me at all. I planned to build a friendship with her because we still had kids to raise, but I knew now was not the time. "Look, if you choose to stick around like I've asked you to, this condo is yours. The least I can do is make sure you and my kids have a home." She looked at me and nodded to let me know she appreciated the gesture. "Well, since I'm still here right now, can you please get your clothes out of the bedroom and leave?" She wasted no time and I couldn't say I blamed her. "Sure." I stood slowly and disappeared into the bedroom. I'd just done one hard thing in the name of finally being honest. Now I needed to talk to Maxwell. "Who is it?" I heard Shanice's voice and almost turned around. "Uh, it's Dan." She opened Maxwell's door slowly and walked away, leaving the door open for me to walk in. "How you doing, Shannie?" I asked, but she ignored the question. "I'll go get Max for you." She seemed different, but I couldn't put my finger on what was wrong with her. She normally glowed with beauty, but today it looked like all of her joy had somehow been stolen. The glimmer of happiness that always just hit you wasn't there. "What you need, bruh?" Maxwell was already on the defense seeing me. "I just want to talk, man, that's it. No drama!" "What you want to talk about? The man your mom hired to attack Shanice? Huh? You want to talk about that? Want to talk about how you pretended to be her friend so your mother could fuck her life up?" I was caught completely off guard. I knew I needed to put some space between us because I knew he was ready to throw down and I didn't come to his house to fight. "Look I don't know what you're talking about, I've barely talked to my mother!" "You think I believe that, man? I should whoop your ass right here right now, but I'm going to give you the chance to leave!" I put my hands up where he could see them so he'd know I wasn't trying to fight him. "Max, come on, man, you know me better than that. You know I would never let anyone hurt Shannie! Calm down! I came over here to apologize to you, and that's it! I don't know anything about any attacks!" He looked at me for a moment and his expression softened a little. "Apologize then." He was staring me down. "Look, man, I'm sorry for all of this Shanice stuff. We said we'd never let some girl come between us and, even though Shanice ain't just some girl, I don't want to let it keep us from being boys." "You sure?" "Yeah, man, I'm sure! I need you, bruh. I've been drowning and ain't had nobody to go to. My mom is playing me, too." The tension in the room was gone just that quick. "You ain't the only one." "Look, all I ask is if we are going to be boys, don't ever talk to me about Shannie." "No worries, bruh! I don't talk to other people about my woman, you know that." We dapped each other up and sat on the couch while I filled him in on the bullshit I'd found out about some nigga named Jamie being my damn daddy.

Chapter 43

SHANICE

I pulled up to my grandmother's house and sighed. It had been a few months since I'd spoken to her. I just couldn't get over all these secrets she seemed to have. I still wanted to know her connection to Dan's mom, but after all that had taken place in my life since the last time we talked, I felt like it might be best I didn't know. If my grandma was as evil as that woman, it would be better if she just kept it to herself. I looked around before I approached the door and the day was gloomy. The clouds were gray and looked as if they could burst with rainfall at any moment. It really matched my mood as of late. Tameka swung the door opened before I could use my key. "Took you long enough!" "I had things to do." "What's been wrong with you lately,

Shannie? You haven't been yourself and you look horrible!" she said as she gave me the once over. I was wearing a pair of gray sweat pants, one of Max's navy blue t-shirts that said Army, and pair of navy and white Jordan 13's. My hair was all over my head and my smile was nonexistent. "Thank you," I responded as I brushed past her. "Well, damn, nobody told me we were having a family reunion today!" I walked in the living room to see Harvey, Sharon, and my grandmother all sitting there laughing and talking. Harvey stood and stared at me as if he was in awe. This man looked like he spit me out himself. Hell, I was in awe. "I have the DNA test results with me. I wanted to open them in front of everyone." His voice was low, but you could still hear the kindness in it. "Okay. Open it!" Tameka chimed in, sounding like she was telling him to open a Christmas present. Just looking at this man, I knew he was our father; there could be no other possibility. He slowly opened the manila envelope and read it to himself. Tears began to flow as a smile formed across his face. "Oh my God! I can't believe I missed out on over twenty years of my children's lives!" He dropped the paper to the floor and put his hands over his face. My grandmother walked over to console him and it pissed me off. "This is your fault. Don't try to console that man now! You told my mother to keep us away from him! To keep us a secret! Do you know how long me and Tameka have needed a father while we were sitting here thinking he didn't want us and all we had was you!" "Shannie!" Tameka yelled my name in an attempt to shut me up. "Shannie, my ass! We have a father and we never knew him because of her. How can you not be mad?" I turned to walk out and was stopped dead in my tracks when I ran into Miss Harris and my mother. Today couldn't get any more interesting, I thought to myself.

Chapter 44

MAXWELL

I sat at my desk with thoughts of Shanice. She'd been going through a hard time with the rape case and, though it had been a couple weeks, she still wouldn't allow me to touch her. I could barely get a laugh out of her. I knew she was angry and lost, I could tell by the way she'd broken down into tears at church on Sunday when the Pastor was preaching about forgiveness. I pulled the ring out of my desk drawer I'd bought her months ago and prayed a proposal would at least take her out of her funk. That it would let her know she had someone who wanted to be her protector forever. I knew it would take some time for her to want me intimately again, but I was willing to wait and would continue to pray for her. I'd allowed my life to get thrown so far off track all because of the love I carried for Shanice that I knew I couldn't let that happen again, I had to secure things between us, and I knew marriage would do just that. Dan and I had talked and everything seemed to be normal with us again, but I still didn't much trust him. I felt he was still hiding something, something big, and I wouldn't trust him until he told me what it was. "Hey, man! Welcome back." Jackson walked into my office and although his mouth said welcome back, his demeanor told me something was up. "Hey! What's up?" He pulled out the chair directly in front of me. "You remember when I told you if something else came up with you that I couldn't call in any favors?" I was confused. I'd been home with Shannie for the past couple of weeks, so I couldn't have gotten into any trouble. "What's going on, man?" "I said I couldn't call in any favors, but I was able to get this one. You're PCSing." "Permanent Change of Station? Why?" "Gabriel Moore. A private, man?" I lowered my head in shame. "For real, bruh. I'm leaving Bragg because of her?" He looked at me like he was shocked I'd said that. "No. You're leaving Bragg because of you. Did you really think you were going to sleep with a private, break it off, and she was still going to keep your little secret?" He shook his head.

"Y'all young cats have a lot to learn. You leave at the end of next month. You're going to Fort Drum." His voice was low, but stern. He got up and walked out of my office. "Thanks, man." I hated that I was going to Fort Drum, but it was much better than a court martial. I just prayed Shanice would be willing to follow me there. I couldn't lose her again.

Chapter 45

DANDRIDGE

"**W**ow! You're my father, huh?" I stood face to face with Jamie, who it took me no time to find. I'd approached him in the Food Lion parking lot and, by the small amount of groceries he carried; I could tell he lived alone. He glared at me. "I don't know you, boy." "You may not know me, but I'm damn sure you know La'Draysha Harris." His entire expression changed. "Bingo!" I said. "How old are you?" he asked. "Twenty-six. You sleep with her twenty-six years ago?" He looked even more stunned. "What month were you born?" "July." "Damnit, Draysha!" he yelled. "She told me there was no way you could be mine." He processed time real fast – most people would have had to count on their fingers, making

156

sure things added up. "Well, I think there is a strong possibility I could be," I said with a straight face. I was tired of my mother and I was going to find out if she'd been lying about who my father was. I loved Dan Senior and always would, but I felt I deserved to know. "Follow me back to my place. We can talk, see where we go from here." He put his groceries in his car and I agreed to follow him. Jamie and I sat down in his small, one-bedroom apartment and I observed all the equipment he had. "Photographer?" I asked. "Something like that." I could tell he wasn't a very open man. "Why did you find me?" "Because I deserve to know who my father is, man!" "Your father is the dude who raised you. I didn't even know you were mine, so I'm nobody to you." He was very cold and blunt. "Why did you have me follow you here if you're just going to go on and on about how you were a sperm donor?" "Look, if you want to get a DNA test, we can do that. I can't promise you a relationship from here on out, but at least everybody will know the truth. I only told you to follow me because I didn't want my ice cream to melt." He lifted up the box of ice cream sandwiches before placing them in the freezer. "You said we could talk and see where to go from here." "What do you want me to say? I could be your father, I can't promise you a relationship, and that's it." He looked annoyed. "You know what, man, don't worry about it." I turned to walk away. If this butthole was my dad, maybe I was better off without him.

Chapter 46

LA'DRAYSHA

The look on Shanice's face when she saw me with her mother was priceless. She stood at the door of Betty Mae's house just staring. The pain behind her eyes made me happy. I knew that pain. It was the look of someone who had been hurt, who'd had something stolen from her. "What are you doing here?" she asked. I laughed. "I came for the family reunion." "Bitch, you aren't family!" I laughed again. "That's what you think." I brushed past her and walked into the house as if I'd been invited. It was about time Betty Mae and I had a reunion. "Nice to see everybody!" I said as I walked into the living room to see Betty Mae, Tameka, Sharon, and Harvey. "La'Draysha!" A smiled formed across Betty Mae's face as she looked at me, almost on the verge of tears. "Please don't act happy to see me." "Melissa?" I could tell Betty was now confused as Melissa and Shanice emerged into the room to join us. Shanice asked the question that was written on everybody's face. "What the hell is going on?" "Why don't you tell her, Betty? Tell everybody how you gave me away. How my life was ruined because of you." "Ruined? You went to a nice family. They certainly had more than I could give you." I saw confusion written across her face. "Don't play stupid, you know those people weren't good people. You let them adopt me and rape me!" I yelled. "Oh my God." She shook her head and sat down. "It was you? You killed those people?" "They got what they deserved for the things they'd done to me." "And to think I tried to find you after that. I heard about their house and that their child had somehow made it out, and I tried to find you." Tears rolled down her cheeks and her fake sympathy made me even more upset. "You liar! You didn't try to find me. I lived right around the corner for over six months. If you had wanted to find me, you could have!" She looked like she'd been bulldozed. "I'm sorry you had to go through that, La'Draysha. I really am." "Apologize to your granddaughter because she knows what it is like, don't you, Shanice?" "I knew it was you! You bitch!" Shanice launched at me and, before I knew it, her hands were wrapped around my neck and Harvey was trying to pull her off of me. "Your grandma let it happen to me, so why not let someone she loves feel my pain!" "It's not my fault you were raped." Betty Mae's voice was barely a whisper as she spoke. "Because of you, my innocence was stolen from me! How can you feel it's not your fault?" "This is why you drugged me?" Melissa finally chimed in. She started to yell. "I was hooked on drugs for years after I got clean, all because you were mad at my mother? What the fuck is wrong with you? I thought you were my friend when we reconnected! You didn't want my mom to know, because you were plotting against this family!" "I took you to rehab so get over it!" I told her. "I was raped because of you! You paid that man to rape me!" Shanice was crying hysterically. "And you! What kind of grandmother are you? I trusted you and you lied to me? To hell with all of you!" She yelled and walked out of the house. "Checkmate!" I said. All I wanted was for Betty Mae's family to stop loving her the way she'd stopped loving me and I'd won! This old lady would die loveless and alone. All these years of planning and I was finally able to see this day. "You're an evil bitch!" Melissa said as she sat beside her mother who looked like she was going to stroke out at any moment just from the shock of everything. "Thank you." I smiled and walked toward the door. I was going to call Tina so we could have a drink and I could celebrate.

Chapter 47

MAXWELL

I looked at Shanice, stunned at everything she'd just told me. It was way too much to take in. All these years of Miss Harris not liking her, literally had nothing to do with her at all. Dan's mom really had some deep-rooted issues. "So what about you and your grandmother? She raised you, Shannie, you can't just give up on the relationship you have with her." "I don't know, Maxwell. I can't trust her. And although I know what happened with Dan's mom is not her fault, she still lied to me and Tameka. All these years we could have actually had a father. How would you feel if you found out your mom lied to you about your father?" "I'd be hurt, but I'd forgive her. I would like to think." I was being honest. I couldn't tell her exactly what

I'd do in her situation, because I hadn't experienced it, but I could tell her what I thought I'd do at the moment. "I don't know. I just don't know. Dan's mom has pretty much ruined my family." "Pray about it, babe," I said. It was the only real solution I could think of. I walked into the kitchen to get dinner started and my phone started ringing. It was the ring that let me know Sharon was calling. Shanice's day had already been long enough, I didn't want to answer Sharon's call and then it end up being some drama, so I hit ignore. "Bae, look at this." Shannie walked into the kitchen showing me her phone which displayed a text from Dan. "Hey Shannie! I really need to talk to you, I have to get some stuff off my chest. Call me." I shook my head. I couldn't believe him. He was still the same ol' Dan, only looking out for him and not wanting to let anyone else to be happy. "Are you going to reply?" "No. But I don't want any secrets between us." "Look, Shannie. I have to tell you something." I sighed because I couldn't keep my transfer to New York to myself any longer. "I'm getting PCSed to Fort Drum, New York. And I want you to come with me." The look on her face almost made me backtrack on my words and try to think of something to say to convince her. "You want me to move to New York with you? I just moved back into your house, Max. This is a big decision. I'm tired of making life-changing decisions for men I'm not even married to." I dropped down on one knee in front of her and pulled the three carat, princess cut diamond ring out of my pocket. "Well, don't make a life-changing decision for someone you're not married to. Make it for your husband. Shannie, every day I spent without you was hell and I do not want to go through that hell again. Will you be my wife?" Tears flowed from her eyes like an endless waterfall as she shook her head yes. I knew we'd have a long road ahead of us, but I was ready to do whatever it took to make things between the two of us work, to make things as perfect as they could be. I picked her up and hugged her as tight as possible and, for the first time since her attack, she allowed me to hold her. "Get your butt to the hospital now, Sharon is in labor!" I read a text right after I put Shanice down. I showed her the text and smiled. "This couldn't have come at a better time, now you'll get to see you left me for no reason." I smiled at her and we headed for the door.

Chapter 48

LA'DRAYSHA

I sat in the waiting room with Tina as she waited for, what she thought was, her grandbaby to be born. Max and Shanice were on their way and so was Dan. I'd called him because, even though this child would never know Dan as his father, he should at least see him before everything hit the fan. Maxwell wasn't stupid. He'd get a DNA test, but no one would suspect my son to be the father, so Sharon would just look like a whore who didn't know who her child's father was. "She had him yet?" Maxwell asked as soon as he spotted us in the waiting room. "No, but the doctor said it should be soon." "Good. I'm ready to get this over with and prove to this girl she's delusional." "Hey, come on." Shanice stopped Max from saying anything more about her sister. I didn't realize she'd accepted her into the family yet. "I'm sorry, Shannie, but your sister is coo coo!" Max said. Harvey ran into the room with Dan right on his heels. It was obvious he was excited to become a grandfather. "Well, looks like this baby has a lot of love," I said in my most sarcastic tone. "Why are you such a bitch?" Harvey caught me off guard with his question. "Aye, man, don't speak to my mother like that." Dan stood up and I knew I might want to tell him to relax before anything escalated. "Calm down, son, it's okay. He's had a long day." I smirked. "Where's the father?" The nurse had come in and all eyes were on Max. "Alleged father," he said as he followed her out of the room. Harvey was confused. "What does he mean 'alleged'?" "He doesn't think it's his," I said before anyone else could and I thanked God no one noticed the look Dan shot me. Dr. Marcus Campbell walked into the waiting room. "Miss Harris! I'm glad to see you. I've been trying to reach you for some time now. We really need to talk. Can you step out?" I rolled my eyes. I knew he just wanted a date. "Sure, Marcus." I stood and followed him to an empty room not too far from the waiting room. "How have you been feeling lately?" he asked. "I've been fine," I lied. I didn't think it was his business that I'd been seeing and talking to my mother. That wasn't his line of work anyway. "That's interesting. Are you sure you've been okay?" He looked at me like he knew I was lying. "Look, Marcus, if you need to say something to me just say it." "Dr. Freeburg passed your records to me because months ago we discovered cancer in your right breast. You've been avoiding my calls and I assume you haven't opened the mail from our office because we haven't seen you for further testing." All of a sudden my head started spinning. This man did not just tell me I had breast cancer. "We need to run some scans and see if it has progressed. You're very lucky, Miss Harris, you haven't noticed signs, this may mean it hasn't spread yet." I heard him talking, but I felt like I was in some sort of twilight state and I'd tuned him out. Cancer? I couldn't believe I had cancer, there were so many things I hadn't done yet. I had to call Jamie and tell him I loved him. I had to get my children together. My eyes filled with tears, I couldn't believe this man just told me I was dying.

Chapter 49

MAXWELL

I followed Sharon's nurse into the nursery where they kept the kids. She led me over to a little boy who wore a bracelet on his leg with Sharon's name on it so they'd know who the child belonged to. "Would you like to hold him?" the nurse asked. "No," I answered as I looked at the little boy in awe. I immediately got angry, realizing this child looked like a spitting imagine of someone I knew. "What do I have to do for a DNA test right away?" I asked, already knowing what the results would be. "Oh, we'll just swab the two of you now and send it to the lab. We'll have the results for you before the child and his mother are discharged," she explained. "What if I know someone else who needs to be swabbed?" "You can call them. It would be better if they had it done now so they don't have to pay later." I walked away without replying as I headed back to the waiting room. "You son of a bitch!" I was in Dan's face before he'd ever saw me coming. Shanice hopped up. "Maxwell, what's wrong?" "How many more secrets are you holding onto, Dan? First, you texting my fiancé telling her y'all need to talk like we didn't just become boys again. And now this shit!" "Your fiancé?" He looked at Shanice like she'd driven a knife through his heart. "Yes, my fiancé!" "Wow!" He collapsed in a chair like someone had just run him over. My mother stood up and placed her hand on my back. "What's going on, son?" "I knew it wasn't my kid, but I didn't expect it to be his!" "I guess the cat's out the bag!" Miss Harris said as she stood at the door looking cold and lifeless.

To Be Continued...

SNEAK PEEK

MY BROTHER'S KEEPER

BOOK IIII

A Novel

Billie Dureyea Shell

Chapter 1

THE GENERAL

The General looked around his office, pondering his next move on the rebels. The rebel army had caused more problems within his smuggling business as of late. While he was out of the country trying to secure the African Black Diamond as his brother, also the South African president, had commanded. The rebels had raided his military artillery camps, taking whatever they could grab. He didn't receive any of the money promised from his brother because he'd failed to bring home the diamond. His next move had to be great, or the president would have his head put on a stake. The General watched people move about through his massive office window. He heard a knock at the door. He didn't bother walking over to ask who was interrupting his time of peace. "It's open, lieutenant." He continued to face the outside world. His mind moved to another place after the death of his father. The diamond was the cause of his murder, and the General would do anything to retrieve the precious stone, even if it meant going against his brother's rule. "General," the lieutenant stepped into the office. "My apologies for interrupting. I've come to ask how you wish to proceed with the rebels?" It was a question that he couldn't avoid with everything that had happened up until this point. Mainly with his brother putting an end to their field supplies. The army needed more weapons to deal with the rebels. He didn't have enough guns to supply all of his men. If he decided to move forward and attack the rebels, some would attend the battle without a weapon to fire. Instead, they would have to make use of knives, grenades, spears, or whatever they could construct to defend themselves. His army outnumbered the rebels, but the outcome would be intensely felt due to the number of casualties they would suffer in a war with another country. If only he had a replacement for Bill Right, the man he knew as Jar Simmons. "How would you like us to deal with the situation, Abrafo?" The General asked his most trusted comrade. For years, they had known each other since they were kids, training to become soldiers in the African military. The General excelled in war strategy while Abrafo exceeded in kills. And that's what his name stands for . . . executioner. The General gave Abrafo his name after learning about his family history. They were assassins, and the name Abrafo suited him well. It was the General's way of protecting his only friend's identity. "You are our leader," Lieutenant Abrafo replied. "It would be wise for you to give the command, not me. I am a man of war, and you are a man of approach. Your tactic will be far more effective than mine." The General turned from the window to face Abrafo. "Do you think it would be wise to start a war with the rebels?" The General wanted to test the lieutenant to see his view of their unfortunate circumstance. It didn't take long for Abrafo to understand what the General asked of him. The General wouldn't ask a third time for his opinion. "No, General." The answer was short, the way he intended for it to be, knowing a why question would follow. "Why do you feel as such?" The General asked curiously. Abrafo didn't become a high-ranking lieutenant by being a cretinous man. The army had to confront the rebels from a different standpoint, and the General needed a fresh perspective. Abrafo was more than a killer to him. He would be the General's new plan of action until his mind was off the diamond. He couldn't lead his men into a war without a clear sense of reason. "The rebels are growing strong in numbers," the lieutenant said evenly. "And they're confident now that they have successfully raided our camps for weapons. We will lose more soldiers than intended if we face them without first breaking their spirit." "Break their spirit," the General folded his hands behind his back. "And how would you suggest proceeding without a battle?" The lieutenant took a short moment to think about an answer. If he replied quickly, the General would possibly void his response. He looked to be deep in thought. His explanation had to be clear of mistakes and thoughtful. He spoke when formulating the right choice of words. "The same way you stop a fire-breathing dragon." The General smiled at Abrafo. "We cut off the head." Abrafo balled his first and placed it over his heart. "For Africa." The General followed suit. "For Africa."

Chapter 2

KANE

"How much longer," Smoke sounded from the seat across from mine. "It's been hours, and my legs feel paralyzed." I looked back at my friend and smiled. Honestly, I was happy he could move his legs at all. Adrian had shot him in the leg, and Smoke had to use a cane to stand up straight for a week. At first, I thought he would never be the same, but that was just me worrying too much. My guy pulled through just fine. "It's not that bad," Kim said. "We'll get there in the next thirty minutes or so. Sit back and relax, crybaby." Smoke threw his head back on the seat rest, frustrated. I shook my head and turned my attention back to the map I had picked up in a store at the airport. We were on our way to Africa. Even Big Bruce decided to come with us. I told him it could get ugly, and he was still down to ride. None of us were in trouble with the law, so I booked a commercial flight straight to Tripoli, Libya. It cost me $1500 a ticket. Not that it mattered, but damn, I know now why people save money for vacations. This was my first time leaving the country, and it felt good to get away even though I was traveling to find my mother. I didn't have my father's black notebook anymore. It would've been helpful because it had names and locations. The only thing I had to lean on was the map in my father's office. There were pinned locations that corresponded with the notebook. That's how I figured out my mother would be somewhere in Libya. It's where my father built his organization and headquarters. Where I assume he stored the money and weapons. The only thing I couldn't figure out was why my mother chose Jordan over me? We could've done this together. "How long are you gonna stare at that map?" Kim asked. "What are you trying to figure out that we don't know already?" "Roads, places," I gave her a short answer. "Studying the landscape." "Why," she asked and leaned her head against my shoulder. "One, I think it'd be best if I at least know where we're at," I informed her. "And two, I'm searching for an unoccupied area away from the city. Somewhere, a plane can land without being noticed by the army." "I thought your father worked with the army?" I looked around and saw several people staring at us. Mostly Africans, heading back to their homeland after visiting America. After Kim said, your father worked with the army; we caught ugly glares from everyone who heard. "Keep your voice down," I whispered. "I don't think foreigners should be talking about the army." She secretly looked around and spotted the people with hard eyes on us. "Right." "Anyway," I began. "I wasn't talking about Libya's army. I was talking about rebel armies who'd love to get their hands on money and weapons. My father would've avoided those areas to prevent any problems." "What if he paid them off," she remembered to speak with a low voice. "It's possible," I said. "But why spend extra money when you can just stay off the grid?" My father wouldn't work with them knowing they were against the army—too much of a headache." "For you," she replied. "I think like him," I smiled. "Whatever, smart guy," she kissed my cheek. I believe it to be true that my father wouldn't work with a malicious group. The notebook had names of Generals and prominent figures written in it. He was larger than life, and it would take more than a few soldiers to protect what he built. He used to tell me, don't work hard at something if you're gonna half-ass in the end? I wouldn't do it, so why would he? The only thing I ever smuggled was contraband from one cell to another when I was locked up. The guards didn't allow inmates to trade anything, so we had to move low-key. I met a guy who would watch my cell while I was on free time for a pack of cigarettes a week. Inmates would sneak into your cell and steal goods while you were away watching TV or occupied in the yard. After it happened to me once, I knew that I had to hire help. I paid a killer to watch over other inmates with sticky fingers, and it worked. This situation was no different. My father hired the army so he could move freely on the land, but that didn't mean the rebels wouldn't try their hand. If you build a restaurant around rats, they'll eat your food. That's how I look at it. And . . . there are plenty of rats where we're going, if you know what I mean.

Chapter 3

ABEL

Abel checked his watch and smiled. Silva had successfully landed the plane in Africa. They had touchdown just past the border of Mali. Abel looked around the area through the side window and saw the desert go on for miles. The sand and dirt covering the area appeared to be endless, and he had already begun to feel the heat beaming down from the sun. He stood when the plane came to a complete stop, opting to sit in the back to keep a close eye on Silva and Britt. "How hot is it?" Gina stood and wiped the sweat from her forehead. The heat made her want to ask Silva to fly them back home. She had never experienced a high temperature at this level, and it was more than enough to get her frustrated. "It's one hundred and five degrees," Snake answered exasperatedly.

"What the fuck," Gina muttered at nobody in particular. "I'm getting woozy," Bam stood and dropped back into the seat. "I don't know if I can do this. It's too hot for me to think straight." Gina formed a disgusted expression on her face when she looked at Bam. It was her moment to comment on his weakness, but receiving a response would've gotten her even angrier in combination with the sun. The heat provided her enough irritation to deal with for now. "Get yourself together," Abel told Bam before opening the plane's side door. He immediately felt a strong breeze of heat attack his entire body as if an unknown entity forced it. The fury of wind lasted a short span before he was able to step off the aircraft. Abel held up his hand and spotted a large dome tent and a 4x4 off-road jeep. The campsite appeared invisible from the air. It was the perfect color for someone who wished to camouflage it with the surrounding landscape. Silva turned off the engine and followed the others off the plane. He stood next to Abel and pointed at the dome tent. "Dat a ih." Mali was the closest destination Silva could land without the army noticing the aircraft. Abel knew this to be true with the amount of illegal activity that had taken place throughout the years. If he desired a safe and secure landing, Mali was the only option without the plane getting shot down. He turned to Bam and Snake. "Unload the supplies." Bam spoke up, "What about her?" his eyes were on Gina, wondering why Abel didn't ask her to help. "Shut up, you idiot," Snake eyed Bam. Abel didn't bother to turn around when he spoke. "I want you to be alive when I return." Bam was mind-boggled with Abel's response. His words rang out in his mind . . . I want you to be alive when I return. Bam planned to murder Gina before leaving America, and he knew that she carried the same intentions. Abel was right. They couldn't be left alone together, not even for a second. He sucked his teeth and followed Snake back inside the plane. Gina smirked at Bam as he turned away, thinking his time would come. Keep on, tough guy, she thought. Hiding her anger toward Bam was becoming a daily task. When Abel no longer needs Bam, he's dead. He was at the top of her to-kill list, without a doubt. Britt stepped beside Abel. "I noticed you're in pain while on the plane. Is everything alright with you?" She had a concerned look on her face. Gina bumped Britt out of her way and stood next to Abel. "He's fine," she snarled. "Let's go inside. It's fucking hot out here." She held Abel's arm and guided him toward the tent. Silva witnessed the tension between Gina and Britt. He was still unaware of how Britt felt about Abel. She hadn't shown any signs of feelings for him until now. "Blurtnawt," he muttered, walking past Britt. Abel stopped at the tent's door, waiting for Silva to catch up and lead the way inside. "After you," he smiled at Silva as if opening the door would spring a trap. "Yah mon," Silva pulled back the opening, showing there was nothing to fear. After stepping inside, he called to the man sitting Indian-style on a throw rug in front of them. "Oyoo." Oyoo opened his eyes and stared at them. He had a mean expression on his face as though they disrupted his concentration while meditating. After a short moment of studying the other unknown guests, he smiled at his friend. "Silva," Oyoo sounded excited and stood to greet him. Abel stood firm by the door with Gina as the two men shook hands. He kept his eyes on Oyoo the entire time while on high alert. If he missed any potential threats, Gina would take care of it. That's why he wanted her to come inside with him. Her awareness was greater than Bam and Snake's put together, which kept him at ease. Oyoo looked over Silva's shoulder and spoke. "That man reminds me of someone. Who is he?" Silva turned around and faced Abel. "Di dead mon son." Oyoo's eyes widened. "Jar," he said in shock. He stepped closer to Abel. "Have you come to take his place?" Oyoo noticed Abel's muscular physique, and the man was by far larger than his father. Oyoo worked with Jar for more than twenty years as a driver. When beginning the smuggling business, Silva and Oyoo were Jar's first transportation hires. Jar cared for them to the point that there wasn't a need to work for anyone else. Even after Jar's death, the men were well off, but they loved making money and stayed in business as contractors for anyone looking to transport. Abel scanned Oyoo as he approached, noticing he was a man of the land who could speak perfect English. He was surprised by that and how well kept it was inside the tent. He expected it to be dusty and hot. It was neither, and somehow the sun rays didn't affect the inside temperature. "I haven't decided as of yet." "Then why have you come, son of Jar?" Oyoo looked at Abel's chest and felt his pain. It was a gift he possessed that allowed him to sense the aura surrounding the body. "I've come for the General," Abel answered truthfully. "I have a gift for him." Oyoo smiled sarcastically. "A gift for the General. The man who brings war to his people." Oyoo turned away from Abel. "What gift do you bring, if not weapons? He values his army, and your father made a business of it. Your gift will get you killed." "I beg to differ," Abel said confidently. "I have something he's been searching for." Oyoo turned around and thought, could he possibly have it? There was only one thing the General would accept besides weapons. And that would be the African Black Diamond. He was well aware of the rebels raiding the campsites. The General announced that anyone who worked with the rebels would be killed. "You have it?" Abel signed with a slight nod. "Okay, I will lead you to the General, but I will not reveal myself," Oyoo said, hiding his true intentions. He pointed to Abel's chest. "I will show you to a doctor before we go. You will need all of your strength, son of Jar."

Chapter 4

JORDAN

Noti looked at the surrounding area and noticed a plane at their landing spot. It's been several years since she returned to the landing zone. It was one of many locations Jar used for travel. She remembered meeting Oyoo with her husband at a bar in Bamako. Oyoo worked as a tour guide and offered to show them around the city. Jar accepted, and the next day Oyoo picked them up from a hotel. They toured the entire town, and Jar was impressed with Oyoo's sense of direction and driving skills. It was enough for Jar to extend a proposal for Oyoo to be part of the business. Noti thought about landing the plane anyway but quickly decided it wouldn't be a good idea. Her husband was dead, and she figured Oyoo had found a new boss. Nobody knew who she was except

Oyoo, and whoever it was visiting might not be friendly. They were in dangerous waters, and steering clear of violence was the key to staying alive a day longer. "We need to land at another location." "I thought this was the location," Adrian spoke up from the pilot's seat. "I don't see anywhere else to land." Rick sat in the back of the plane next to Jordan. He'd never been more terrified in his life. Jordan and his brother Adrian were monsters. After Jordan woke up, he became himself again, and the FBI agent was gone. He lashed out at Adrian for knocking him over the head. Adrian could've wrecked the plane if Noti and Rick didn't stop him in time. Jordan kept his eyes on his brother for most of the trip. Rick thought if he closed his eyes for a second, they all be dead. Sleep was not an option either, and he damn near didn't blink. "Land this fucking plane," Jordan growled at Adrian. "You said this was the spot, and now you've changed your mind all of a sudden. That's not gonna work for me. This flight is over." He stared at Noti hard. She somehow became the bandleader, which didn't sit right with him. She'd be useless if he could get her to give up the safe location and the passcode. Striking that kind of luck would end her life, and he knew it wouldn't happen. He'd never get the information, not if she desired to live. Jordan's frustration dictated his actions, and until he regained control of the situation, his goal was to piss them off. "Never mind the plane," Noti said evenly. "And prepare yourself for a fight. That's the only option if we land now." "She's right," Rick spoke up. He noticed the aircraft and spotted two men unloading luggage. "Well, we have to land soon," Adrian checked the gasoline level meter. "We're running short on fuel." They had to miss a fuel station because a police boat docked nearby. He couldn't risk it and let the last opportunity pass by. Jordan began to spaz out, letting his emotion run wild. "Fuck!" he roared and started to destroy anything in reach. "How are we runnin' short on fuel?" He tossed random items to the front of the plane. He picked up a glass of water and threw it at the front window, just missing Adrian. "Goddammit!" "Someone calm his ass down," Adrian shouted and took a split second to glance back at Jordan. That would've been the last straw if the glass hit him. Jordan was pushing it to the maximum limit, and Adrian was more than ready to do something harmful to his brother, even if it meant ending his arrangement with Noti. Rick turned his attention from the plane below and focused on his former partner. "Shit," he muttered and tried to defuse Jordan's outrage. He held up his hands and blocked Jordan from throwing more items toward the cockpit. "Are you trying to kill us?" "Get the hell out of my way, Rick." Jordan had the devil inside of him and wasn't afraid to show it. The Planner was the cause of his outrage. It wasn't his fault the plane was running out of fuel. It wasn't his fault Noti was the one in control. It wasn't his fault Rick had to tag along with them. So many different things began to fester inside his head, and he wanted to break loose. Freeing himself from everyone and unleashing his anger was the only way to do it. It made him feel good, and Rick kept trying to stop that sensation. "I can't let you distract your brother from landing this plane safely." Rick kept his hands up and continued to block Jordan's path. Why did I get myself into this, he thought. He wouldn›t be in this predicament if he only called for backup when discovering the cabin. Obey the rules as an officer and follow protocol. That's all it takes, and he failed to do both when Adrian apprehended him in the woods. Jordan suddenly felt exhausted, and he just stood there, staring at Rick like a madman. His chest heaved in and out, taking in deep breaths of air. He needed water before he passed out from dehydration. It was hot, and his energy output didn't agree with the heat from the sun. He looked at the cooler on the side of the seat. Hopefully, there was another bottle of water inside. He reached for it, and Rick reacted by moving in his way. "Get the hell out of my way. I need a drink." Rick sighed and looked at the cooler. "Okay," he moved to the side. Jordan opened the cooler and cracked open a water bottle. He tossed the cap at Rick's chest, and it bounced off to the ground. He smirked at him, "Rookie." The whole time Jordan was having a fit, Noti focused on the plane below. The men appeared to be Americans. Maybe they were smugglers who prospered after her husband's death. When a king is dead, a new one will rise in any case. The luggage couldn't carry the number of weapons it takes to feed one rebel group. There could be a second plane, or money was in the bags. Suddenly, a woman and Oyoo emerged from the tent. Her eyes were sharp enough to assure it was him. She learned to see from a flying distance in the beginning stages of Jar's operation. He wasn't the only one taking risks for their future. It can't be, she thought. Another figure emerged from the dome tent. Noti was stunned after realizing a demon had followed her to Africa. As the plane passed over the location, she could've sworn Abel looked into the aircraft and made eye contact with her. She fell back from the window in shock. Her heart rate began to speed up a notch, and she felt like it would explode. Abel could have caused her to have a mild heart attack. She put her hand over her chest in fear. Rick caught her from falling to the ground before speaking to her worriedly. "Are you okay?" "No," she answered seriously. "The devil has arrived."

A Novel

Billie Dureyea Shell

Chapter 1

MAXWELL

When she walked into the room, the smell of her sweet perfume struck me and held me hostage. I watched her move about the penthouse as if they were the only two people here. She wore one of his button-up shirts, a pair of socks, and some boy shorts... nothing I'd allow my lady to wear while walking around in front of my boys. But, my boy Dandridge was different... very confident that his woman was his, and she would never stray. He'd been dating her since our ninth grade year in High School, and I must admit that I'd always been jealous because I'd known and liked her since 2nd grade, but she never noticed me. Even right now, she seemed to be looking straight through me as I sat in their living room, staring at her every move. She sat on his lap and kissed him; I immediately felt myself get angry. "Did you come in here for something?" he asked her, as soon as their kiss had ended. "Just to tell you I love you!" she quipped. "You and Max can finish what you're doing. I'll be in the kitchen making dinner." She was everything. She cooked, she helped their maid keep the house clean, and I'd never heard a negative word come out of her mouth toward him. Dandridge had it made, and he barely acted like he knew it. He played basketball overseas for a team in Spain. He called home quite often to tell me about the women over there, and how his celebrity status always landed him the baddest of them, when he should have been taking the time to notice the bad woman he had at home. Shanice was about 5'6" with a beautiful caramel complexion; her smile was enough to give a man a heart attack on his most confident day. She was shaped like a coke bottle, with curves in all the right places, and her eyes were the prettiest shade of grey I'd ever seen. She had beautiful long curly hair, which I was sure came from her father's side of her family because he was a white man. But no matter where her beauty came from, I was mesmerized every time I saw her. How could a man cheat on a woman as perfect as she was? "So how does it feel to be back, man?" Dan asked, drawing me back from my thoughts. "It's alright... just getting used to being around more often. Looking for a place right now," I answered. "I love moms

...but I'm not big on living with her." My mother loved the fact that I was stationed at Fort Bragg. It was only 30 minutes from her house and whenever I wasn't deployed, she'd allowed me to stay at home, which had saved me a lot of money over the past five years. I was able to pay cash for my ride, a 2014 yellow Camaro, and since I'd gotten back from my second deployment, I was finally looking to buy a house. The only thing I hated was that, while I was advancing in my career and education, I didn't have anyone to share it with. Within the next three months, I'd be pinned Captain, and I'd be finished with my master's program ...and the only woman standing beside me would be my mother. "Finally getting away from mom-dukes! I'm proud of you, becoming a man and shit," he smiled, knowing how I would respond. There was a twinkle in his eye as he flashed me a smile, letting me know he was only teasing. Dandridge had been my best friend so long, he could get away with saying that ...but he also knew when to draw the line. "Watch yourself ...I've been a man. I pay rent there," I corrected him. "I'm not just mooching off of my mom." "I was only joking... chill," he said, looking at me apologetically. Before I could respond, his phone started to vibrate. I glanced over and saw the picture of a beautiful woman displayed on his screen. Underneath the image, I could see the words "The Wife" instead of a name on the caller-id. I had no idea what my boy was getting into, but I knew that, whatever it was, it couldn't be good for Shanice. He excused himself and stepped outside to take the call. "Hey Max, do you want another beer?" Shanice asked, poking her head out of the kitchen, her voice holding me captive for a moment. It was the sweetest voice I'd ever heard, one that I wanted to hear for the rest of my life. There was nothing I didn't love about this woman. "No. I'm okay, Shanice. Thank you," I answered her thoughtfully. "Actually, can you let Dan know I'll get back with him later? I have to run." "Yea, sure," she responded, "I'll tell him. See ya." She patted me on the shoulder, keeping a respectable distance while I secretly enjoyed her fragrance. I couldn't sit there thinking about her being done wrong, and I knew I couldn't have this conversation with him while she was home, so I thought it would be best if I just left, but I would definitely be talking to Dan about the woman whose picture I'd seen on his caller-id. We were boys; we didn't really have many secrets.

Chapter 2
DANDRIDGE

"Look, you know I spend summers at home with my family," I argued with Cecilia. I'd married her two years ago because I enjoyed the thought of having a family stateside as well as having a woman to come home to when I was in Spain. Initially, I'd had no intentions of marrying her ...until I found out she was pregnant with my daughter Danielle. I'd planned on coming home after that season, and coming clean to Shanice about my family, but I could never bring myself to leave her, or tell her something that I knew would kill her inside. She'd been down for me since the ninth grade; no matter what I'd done or what mistakes I made, she never left me. She only loved and encouraged me. "I know, baby," she whined into the phone, "but we miss you ...and I hate going through another pregnancy alone." She dropped a bomb on me! I never wanted kids, never really wanted a wife, and now she was telling me she was pregnant again! "You're pregnant? I thought you'd gotten on birth control! Damnit, Cecilia!" I wanted to curse her out from here to next Sunday, but she was my wife and a woman. My mother raised me to always respect women, especially the one I married. "I thought you'd be happy." She began to cry in an effort to gain my sympathy, but it wasn't working; I needed some time. "Call me tomorrow... I can't talk to you right now." "I love you," she whispered meekly, knowing our conversation would end this way. I forced the words she wanted to hear. "Yeah ...you too," I mumbled as I hung up the phone and tried to regain my composure. How would I explain to Shanice that I would have to go back to Spain early? I loved my time at home with her, and how understanding she was every time I left to go play ball, but I didn't feel like she'd understand an early departure. I put on my best game face as I walked back into the house. I could smell the aroma coming from the kitchen, reminding me of one reason why I loved Shanice so much... the girl could cook her ass off. She'd finished the whole culinary thing, but quit her job as head chef of a very high end restaurant when I told her I wanted to take care of her, and she'd been my stay at home girlfriend ever since. "Umm... sure does smell good in here," I bragged as I grabbed her around the waist from behind, looking over her shoulder into the pot to see what was cooking. "I try," she responded as she turned to kiss me. All I could do in the moment was stare into those beautiful eyes. I had a good woman; I really didn't want to leave early. "What's on your mind?" she questioned, sensing I was troubled. "Nothing... just thinking about how much I love you, and how I want to give you everything you desire and deserve to have," I answered her honestly. "Not everything," she countered. I was not prepared to argue with another woman about the same thing. "Here we go," I sighed, knowing I wasn't in the right mood for this discussion. "Shanice, we've talked about this. I just don't want to be anybody's daddy! I want to know that we can do whatever we want, and not have to worry about a babysitter or kids holding us back. I have explained this a million times." "Yeah, I know," she spoke, the sadness in her voice hurting me to my core. I couldn't continue to lie to her, but I also couldn't lose her by telling the truth.

Chapter 3

MAXWELL

"Hi, I'm Sharon," the realtor said as she smiled broadly, extending a well-manicured hand to greet me. We had spoken numerous times on the telephone but this was our first face to face encounter. "Maxwell," I responded quickly, introducing myself while trying to mask my surprised look. She was sexy as hell and I had feeling that when Dan finally showed up, he'd hit on her, but I could tell that she was already checking me out. I was a far cry from the geeky pecan tan mixed guy no one ever really paid attention to in High School, and truth be told, I could pretty much get any female I wanted. There just weren't any that compared to Shanice. "Do you know how long your friend will be? I have another appointment in a few hours. I don't want to be late,"

14

she fretted, glancing around as if she were looking for Dan. "About 10 minutes... he's stuck in traffic on I-40," I informed her, wishing she was a little more relaxed. "Oh okay," she mumbled, but the words didn't match her body language. She was obviously feeling stuck in an awkward position. I'd never been a real big talker, but I figured a little conversation wouldn't hurt to lighten the mood until Dan arrived. I looked at my large feet, and noticed a pebble. Kicking it across the drive, I couldn't help but wonder what made this girl tic. More than just nervous, she lacked the confidence needed in the real estate business. How could a woman so beautiful be insecure? "So, Sharon, are you from here?" I asked, breaking the uncomfortable silence. "North Carolina, yes... but Fayetteville, no. I'm from Greensboro... moved here when I started going to North Carolina Central," she responded quickly, as if relieved that I had asked a question first. She'd given me more information than I'd asked for, though. I never understood why women did that. You ask a simple yes or no question and they give you details on why they said yes or why they said no. I just wanted her to simply answer my question. "Sounds good," I responded. What else could I say? I eyed her for a moment, taking in her 5'4" height, flawless brown skin, beautiful almond shaped eyes, and very pretty smile. She was also dressed to kill, which I find very attractive, so why wasn't I interested in what she had to say? "You seem nervous," I added, deciding to challenge her a little. "Oh no, I'm not nervous," she lied, "just anxious to show the house is all." Looking into her eyes, I knew she was attracted to me because it was very hard for her to act natural. Maybe this girl's not insecure at all... Before I could respond, the moment disappeared with the arrival of Dan's white on white 2013 Yukon Denali. His music was loud as always, blaring Jay-Z's Run This Town ft. Rihanna. Dan seemed go for the 'I need attention' effect in everything he did. "Hey! Sorry I'm late," he said, stepping out of the car to extend his hand to Sharon. "I'm Dan." I'd seen that smile enough times to know that he'd be laying on the charm for this girl. Resisting the urge to shake my head in disapproval, I responded before Sharon had the opportunity. "It's cool Bruh, come on. Let's look at this house." Sharon led us into the beautiful four bedroom, three and a half bath, plantation style home, it's modern touches included hardwood floors, black granite counter tops, a range stove, and luxury his and hers shower heads in the master bath. It was a home fit for the family I planned to have one day. "Why would you buy a house this big, man?" Dan asked, looking at me as if my viewing this home was one of the craziest things he'd ever heard, "it's just you..." "I do plan to have a wife and kids one day," I explained, looking at Dan as if he were crazy. Was he serious ...or just trying to be smooth in front of this girl? I wanted to say something else to defend myself but he continued. "You don't think you should wait till that happens so your wife can pick out your family home with you?" His question made sense, I guess, but since when did Dan start thinking of what his wife would want, anyway? "Sharon, what do you think? Do you think I should go smaller and then upgrade when I find a wife?" I could tell I'd caught her off guard, including her in our conversation but I wanted insight from a female perspective. "I personally wouldn't mind moving into a home my man already purchased, especially if it was a home as nice as this. That's one less thing we'd have to worry about financially." She smiled and I almost melted. "Whatever, man! You think you want a wife and kids one day, but it's not all it cracked up to be. Buy your invisible family this house if you want to," Dan sounded like a bitter, jaded old man. He threw his hands up and walked swiftly into the other room. Something was obviously bothering him. I asked Sharon to give me a minute to look through the house again, although I'd already made up my mind. I just needed time to speak to my boy. He'd been easy to find, standing on the veranda with one hand on his hip and the other leaned against the pillar. "What's up, man? What do you know about having a family?" I asked. "Sure, you've got Shanice, but that's hardly the same as a wife and kids." "I messed up, bruh! I messed up bad... and the situation is getting harder and harder to keep under control." He put his hand to his forehead to think, but then brought it down again as if trying to regain his composure. "What situation?" I could tell by his nervousness and body language that whatever he had gotten himself into wasn't good, but I wasn't prepared for his response. "I married a girl in Spain," he confessed. "We have a two year daughter and now, there's a baby on the way." "You're joking!" I responded, laughing because I honestly thought he was joking until I saw the look in his eyes. "I wouldn't play about nothing like this, man," he hissed quietly, looking behind me to make sure no one could hear, "but the problem is, my family has never really approved of Shanice. They love Cecilia and our daughter... but I love Shanice more than life, bro." His eyes looked watery, as if he were on the verge of tears. "If you loved her, you wouldn't be in this predicament, man," I replied, knowing my words would fall on deaf ears. He was obviously distraught but there was no real remorse in his voice. I honestly wanted to beat him to a bloody pulp but controlled the anger I felt. "You need to tell her the truth." "I can't do that... I can't hurt her like that," he whined, sounding more and more selfish with each word he spoke. He'd rather live a double life than allow Shanice to have the love and happiness she deserved. "I just have to figure out how to tell her I'm leaving for Spain in three weeks because I can't let my wife go through this pregnancy without me!" Before I could say anything, Sharon stepped onto the veranda. "So, have you decided yet?" she asked politely. Dan looked away, smoothing his collar and trying to compose his thoughts. "Yes, I'm going to put in an offer," I announced. It seemed as if my invisible family might materialize sooner than I had originally expected.

Chapter 4

DANDRIDGE

I looked up at the ceiling while Shanice slept peacefully on my chest. I didn't know how I had allowed myself to get into this situation. Caught between two women I cared deeply for, and destined to hurt the one I loved most. Shanice was an amazing woman and she deserved the world, but I knew I'd never be able to give her all that she wanted ...because I'd mistakenly given it to another woman. My relationship with Cecilia started out as a 'friends with benefits' situation. I'd come back to my hotel room one night and she had been a gift from the boys, but there was something different about her. She was beautiful and actually very smart. The first night we spent together, we stayed up late, talking until we fell asleep, and made love in the morning. Cecilia had done some things to me that I only dreamed Shanice would do, but because I was the only man Shanice had been with, she was still rather conservative, which was the only reason I'd sleep with other women. I started inviting Cecilia to home games and bringing her along for the away games. We connected in an indescribable way. I had never considered her my girlfriend but when she popped up pregnant, my mother told me that I needed to leave Shanice alone, and make an honest woman out of the Cecilia, the woman having my child. So, I proposed and two months before she'd given birth to Danielle, we had a small wedding with only our closet family members... none of our friends had been invited. I was still shocked to this day that no one in my family had taken it upon themselves to tell Shanice, but my sister has always said it was my place to be honest with her ...not anyone else's, even though my mom seemed anxious to tell her. I looked down at Shanice. She was so beautiful, sleeping like there was no place she'd rather be. I knew this wasn't the time, but I had to wake her and tell her the truth ...before I lost my nerve. "Yes?" she said without opening her eyes when I shook her awake. I would have found that comical if the situation were different. She's always been bad about answering when she's still sound asleep. "Wake up, babe," I said kindly, urging her to open her eyes, "I need to talk to you." "Now?" she asked quietly. I could tell by her voice that she was bothered that I'd chosen to wake her. "Yes, it's important." She lifted up off of me and propped herself on one elbow so she could face me as I spoke. The moonlight shone through the window, adding the perfect reflection of light. Now that I was able to see those beautiful grey eyes of hers, I lost my nerve. "Okay babe, you have my attention," she said, realizing that I hadn't said anything yet. My thoughts stumbled, looking for the words that would send her back into a peaceful sleep. "I just wanted to say I love you more than life itself, and no matter what, I never want to lose what we have. I never want to lose you." "And you never will," she answered sweetly, "as long as you're always honest with me and faithful to me." She looked at me as if searching for clues of deceit and betrayal. "I would never lie or cheat," I lied. Trying to lighten the mood, I added with a grin, "you've been down for a nigga for too long." "You better not," she said in her most menacing tone as she leaned in and gave me the sweetest kiss. I loved this woman... she was every man's dream.

ABOUT THE AUTHOR

New York Times & International Best Selling Author
Billie Dureyea Shell was born in Compton California and now
lives in Ladera Heights with his wife and
kids who he loves to spend time with.
He is the Owner of several properties in the Los Angeles area
and gives back to his community by providing low income
housing to those who need it.
He stated "It doesn't matter where you at or where you from
it's what you do with your time. There's nothing you can't do
if you put your mind to it".

www.ingramcontent.com/pod-product-compliance
Lightning Source LLC
Chambersburg PA
CBHW072126300726

48975CB00003B/945